Heartquake

A Psychological Suspense

Marci Wilson

MaHanna Press

A Note from the Author

Hey you! If you aren't familiar with my work, welcome! For those who've stuck around through all the ups and downs, welcome back.

My writing journey has had more twists and turns than a soap opera love triangle during sweeps week. And I would know—I sharpened my teeth writing *One Life to Live* fanfiction.

My first publications were erotic titles under the name Emilia Mancini. Then I pivoted to romance as Marci Boudreaux. After that, I signed a contract, was rebranded as Marci Bolden, and spent some time focusing on women's fiction.

Things didn't go as well as I'd hoped, so here we are: incarnation number four—*Marci Wilson*.

This one will stick. Pinky swear.

The name Wilson comes from my great-grandmother, part of a long line of strong, fierce women who survived the unimaginable. I am determined to honor their legacy and carry that strength forward.

Like my foremothers, life has taught me some hard truths—about trust, loyalty, and the very real hazards of doing business with "friends." But now I'm older, wiser, and no longer biting into poisoned apples just because they're being handed to me by someone I *should* have been able to trust.

I've learned that people-pleasing only pleases everyone else. That wolves can wear sheep's clothing for years before showing their teeth. And that there are those who would rather see you fail than celebrate your success if they can't take the credit.

But I've also learned that I'm a fighter. When push comes to shove, I push back. My voice might tremble when I speak up for myself, but damn it, I *will* speak up.

These days, my circle is smaller. My goals are quieter. I trust a little less, give a little less, and protect my wellbeing a whole lot more. I no longer force connections that aren't working.

Funny thing is, readers I've never met have shown me more loyalty and kindness than some people who should have been in my corner all along. And I've made peace with that.

Thank you for walking this new path with me. I promise this version of me will be the best one yet.

—Marci *Wilson*

For everyone who has stood by me during some of the toughest times of my life, even if you didn't know that's what you were doing.

Chapter One

S he missed him. He'd only been gone for three days, but she missed him. The way his blue eyes sparkled when he laughed and the way he said her name. Janis wasn't a romantic name by most standards, but he made it sound poetic. When he spoke, his deep timbre rolled through her, and she could swear he'd set off an earthquake in her heart.

A *heartquake*.

And she felt the aftershocks every time she thought of him.

She missed him. Even though she shouldn't.

Especially since he was on his honeymoon with her little sister.

"*Janis*," her mom said with a sharp tone.

Jan stopped staring out the window at the waves swelling across the waters of *Behía de Banderas* and blinked several times before offering a soft smile. "Sorry. This view has a way of distracting me."

"Don't apologize to *me*." Her mother gestured toward

the man standing at their table.

The familiar burn of embarrassment torched Janis's cheeks as the waiter gave her a slight bow. Though she wouldn't classify his smirk as condescending, it wasn't warm either.

"It's one of the best views in Puerto Vallarta." He smiled but never took the tip of his ink pen from the small pad of paper in his hand. He was trying to be nice, but the impatience in his dark eyes betrayed him.

Eyes had a way of revealing what a person was trying to hide.

Looking at her mother too long was like staring into a mirror that only reflected her flaws. Teachers' gazes seemed to linger on her, silently asking why she never raised her hand. Her classmates looked at her like she was an enigma they didn't care enough to solve. People's eyes carried assumptions, questions, suspicions—like the waiter's just now, as if he could tell how her thoughts had wandered to places they shouldn't. As if he knew she was sitting in paradise, tormented by feelings that she couldn't confess.

She turned her attention to the fake leather portfolio holding a list of dinner options. Anything to keep her eyes down and her feelings buried.

"*Pulpo a la brasa*, please." Janis said each word deliberately so she didn't mispronounce her order.

He scribbled on his pad, took her menu, and then rushed away.

"What?" Janis asked at the frown that had formed on her mother's lips.

"Since when do you like octopus?" Eunice, Janis's older—by two minutes—sister, asked. The doctors had told their mother they were identical, and sometimes they actually did look alike. But Eunice had always been prettier. She knew how to dress and apply makeup and style her hair. She knew how to talk to people and make them laugh. She knew how to stand out in a crowd.

Janis didn't know any of those things.

She ran her hand over the bright yellow dress her twin had encouraged her to wear. Though Eunie said she looked nice, Janis felt like an overripe banana. She preferred to wear muted colors, glasses instead of contacts, and other than an occasional trim to keep her wavy long brown hair healthy, rarely visited a salon. She didn't wear makeup or dye her hair.

And she'd never liked octopus.

But Thomas did.

The night before the wedding, when they were all at dinner, he'd ordered the dish. She hadn't realized what it was. She'd been too distracted by how the sun had tanned his skin and made his straight white teeth brighter than usual. Thomas and Susan had arrived days before everyone else to make certain everything was ready for their destination wedding. The sun had been kind to him.

Janis turned to see where the waiter had gone. Maybe she could call him back and change her order. He was long gone. She swallowed and looked across the table to offer her mom a shrug. "I thought I'd try it again. I'm sure the octopus is much better here." She waved her hand at the bay, as if that would somehow change the taste and texture of the cephalopod. "They get it from right here, don't they?"

"Doubt it," her mom stated with a frown. She narrowed her eyes as if trying to see through to Janis's deepest darkest secrets.

Janis looked away. She hated when her mother stared at her like that—sharp, unblinking, like she was peeling back skin to see what Janis was really made of. Phylis's gaze wasn't curiosity. It was judgment. Cold and clinical, as if she were trying to catch Janis in the act of being something she shouldn't be. Something other than Eunice.

Those calculated stares made Janis' stomach twist. Even now, as an adult, that stare could reduce her to a child again—squirming, ashamed, wrong without knowing why.

She turned her attention to her twin, seeking refuge, but Eunice's eyes mirrored the same expression. Wary. Watching. Like they were both waiting for Janis to slip, to reveal herself.

She blinked, heart skipping, and looked down at her hands instead. This was why she had such a hard time maintaining eye contact. It was never a glance. It was an x-ray. A searchlight. A scalpel.

When people looked at her for too long, she felt like they were digging for things she didn't want them to find—weaknesses, flaws, secrets she hadn't yet named even to herself.

It was safer to focus on details. A wrinkle in a sleeve. The swirl of cream in coffee. Anything but their eyes.

She'd learned long ago that holding someone's gaze meant risking exposure.

And Janis had spent her entire life mastering the art of not being seen—even in plain sight.

"You've been acting odd ever since you got here," Eunie stated before she sipped from her ice water with two slices of lemon.

Janis looked up in time to watch the clear straw fill

with liquid and Eunice cock a brow at her in the way she did right before picking her twin apart.

"She's right," their mom added.

Janis dared to turn her face to her again. "To dinner?"

Eunice let out an exacerbated sigh, as if she couldn't handle Janis's petulance a moment longer. "To Mexico."

Janis returned her attention to her twin who had cocked a thin brow, turning her pretty face into something closer to condescending.

What does her husband see in her? Janis thought. Not much apparently. Since he tended to do everything he could to get away from her. Roger had used the kids as an excuse to stay back in Kansas, but Janis suspected the truth: he needed a break. A reprieve from Eunice's constant micromanaging, her need to control every breath in the room. Janis couldn't blame him.

After setting her glass down, Eunice pursed her lips and Janis braced herself for the incoming storm.

They were scrutinizing her. Determining the most effective way to tear her down.

Panic fluttered in her chest, sharp and sudden, making her heart skip a beat. Her skin felt too tight, like it didn't belong to her. She curled her hands into fists in the folds of the yellow fabric, digging her short nails into her palms, trying to fight the urge to run.

She hated being judged. Especially by her mom and sister. Their cruelty knew no bounds. Nothing was off-limits. No comment too mean or ugly.

"I thought you were nervous about the wedding, but that was over days ago," her mom continued. "Something else is bothering you."

No. It *was* the wedding.

Janis had flown to Mexico to stand next to Susan as she married Thomas. The man who had occupied Janis's thoughts from the first time she'd met him. The man she never should have let into her head, let alone her heart.

Her stomach turned. Even thinking about her feelings was wrong. She was certain something rotten had taken root inside her. Thomas was her brother-in-law now. Her sister's husband. That fact should've been enough to stop the thoughts, the feelings, the what-ifs.

But it wasn't.

Her mom and Eunie had been the ones who had insisted that they stay for a week's vacation to make the cost worth it. Janis hadn't even wanted to attend the wedding. She didn't like flying. Or the beach. Or being someplace new. And she definitely didn't like watching the man of her dreams marry someone else.

Susan had begged her, and Eunie insisted Janis would have been a jerk to refuse. Though, she supposed being in love with Susan's husband also made her a jerk—even if she couldn't control how she felt.

She hated herself for how she felt. Hated the way her heart ached for a man she could never have. She'd told herself how wrong it was to have feelings for him, how much it would hurt Susan if she ever found out, but that didn't seem to matter to Janis's heart.

Susan thought her hesitancy was because she'd always played the so-called second fiddle to Eunice. Therefore, Susan had convinced Janis to not only attend but to be her maid of honor.

Janis had no chance of disappearing into the background. No chance of escaping the happy glow that radiated from the couple or the knowing glances and romantic setting where they vowed to love each other 'til death did them part.

So, yes, it was the wedding bothering her. Hearing Thomas's deep voice repeating vows that spoke to her soul, vows that he'd said to another woman, had burned her more than the scorching Mexican sun on her pale skin and cut her deeper than her twin's cruel comments.

"Susan's right," Eunie said with that judgmental tone she had mastered years ago. "You don't like him."

"Don't like who?" Janis tried to sound innocent. Confused. Like she hadn't been slowly dying ever since Susan and Thomas had gotten engaged.

Leaning forward, her mom dipped her chin. Her eyes filled with accusation. "Thomas."

Janis almost laughed at the suggestion. Didn't like Thomas? If only. Then maybe she wouldn't feel like a traitor every time she looked at Susan.

Ever since she'd met the man three years ago, she'd been under some spell that wouldn't let her go. Susan had brought him home for Thanksgiving and when he'd walked into the kitchen, his broad shoulders filling the doorway and his bright smile shining like a million stars, Janis had nearly fainted. She'd had to grasp the edge of the counter to stop herself from falling into him.

She'd never felt anything like that before. So, she did what any good sister would do. She avoided that man like the plague. Avoided eye contact, avoided conversation, avoided breathing too deeply when he was nearby because his aftershave was intoxicating.

"I never said that," Janis insisted. Because she never had and never could say she didn't like Thomas. Like the fool that she was, she loved him. Quietly. Hopelessly. She loved him in ways she couldn't explain. To anyone. So she buried her affection for him like she'd buried so many feelings before. In a box, sealed tight, and on a shelf deep in the recesses of her mind—only, for some reason, that box refused to stay sealed. "Why would she think that?"

Her mom cocked one overly drawn brow at her. She'd spent so many years plucking the hairs into a barely visible line that they now refused to grow back even though fashion beckoned them to. Instead, she filled the would-be brow with artistic lines that almost looked real. *Almost.* But upon closer inspection, it was obvious they were fake. Like everything else about her. "Because you never speak to him. Never look at him."

Eunie added, "And you can't change the subject fast enough when he comes up."

"I'm shy," Janis said quickly. Too quickly. "You know that."

Her mom shook her head. "He's a very nice man, Jan. Your sister is lucky to have him."

She knew that. She didn't say so out loud, but the truth was like a cement block on her chest. Susan was luckier than any one woman should be—beautiful, smart, successful . . . and happily married.

"What is it about him that you don't like?" her mom pressed.

Janis's throat tightened and her pulse started to thump in her ears. She knew this feeling. Her mom and twin sister were circling, closing in. Her mouth went dry as she prepared for the impending attack. "I never said I didn't like him."

Janis turned to their mother. Phylis was watching her, the way she always had—with eyes that once cut clean and sharp, now clouded with age. Cataracts, maybe. Or simply time, dulling everything.

Her once-rigid posture had softened into a slight stoop. Her hair, gray now, frizzed at the ends where it used to fall pin-straight. The deep lines across her brow and along her mouth hadn't softened with time—they'd sharpened, fossilized into permanent disapproval.

She'd be sixty-nine soon.

Janis tried not to dwell on that. But it was hard not to, especially when her mother looked at her like this—like the same girl who didn't want to go to prom, or audition for the school play, or do anything else that might make her visible. Embarrassing. A disappointment.

Phylis had always been a presence—opinionated, critical, impossible to please. But she'd never been helpless.

Now, she was inching closer to it every day.

Janis swallowed hard. The resentment flared beneath the surface, hot and tight in her chest. Because even now, even after everything, her mother still looked at her with that same weary expectation, like Janis owed her something. Love. Obedience. Grace.

Janis wasn't sure she had any of that left.

"Listen," Phylis began, her voice flatter than usual.

"Mom," Janis interrupted, trying to keep her tone steady. "I love my sister. I'm happy for her."

But her eyes flicked back to Eunie—and what she saw made her stomach turn.

The gleam in her twin's eye wasn't curiosity. It was certainty.

Eunie had figured it out.

And if there was one thing Eunie had never mastered, it was discretion. She wouldn't keep Janis's secret. She would wait, bide her time, and when the moment was right, she'd strike—mercilessly.

Shame surged through Janis, a flood of heat and humiliation that lodged itself deep in her ribs. She felt exposed. Seen.

And not in the way she'd ever wanted.

The other thing Eunie wasn't good at was being kind. People praised her generosity—Eunie the saint, always the helper, always the fixer.

Janis knew better.

Behind closed doors, her sister was sharper than shattered glass and twice as dangerous.

Of all the bullies Janis had faced in her life—and there had been plenty—Eunie was the worst. She knew where to aim and how hard to hit.

Janis's stomach knotted as her mom said something about how wonderful she thought Thomas was. Usually, Janis would hang on the words of anyone complimenting him, but she couldn't hear over the pounding of her heart. Her throat burned, bitter and hot, as bile surged upward. She did what she could to avoid Eunie's constant glances as their mother chattered on and on.

Soon, a plate of octopus was placed in front of Janis and the bile in her throat burned higher. She swallowed hard as she examined the rows of glistening suction cups covered in spicy sauce. Though the dish had been prepared with obvious care, nothing about the meal was appealing.

She really did hate octopus.

Chapter Two

"Walk with me," Eunie said after they got their mom settled in the hotel room they were sharing for the night. "I need a smoke."

"I don't like to be around cigarettes," Janis told her. "You know that."

Their mom chimed in from where she'd buried herself in pillows and blankets in the queen size bed Janis had been forced to share with her since arriving in Mexico. "Go, Jan. I don't want her out there alone."

Out there was the street outside of the hotel since they didn't allow smoking on the grounds. Janis wanted to argue, but she didn't. She never did. Eunie always got her way.

Add that to the long list of things Janis hated about her.

They made it to the elevator before Eunie turned and crossed her arms. Janis did her best to ignore her as Eunie let out a long breath and shook her head.

"If you tell me that you have a crush on our sister's

husband . . ."

Janis looked at her twin, wide-eyed and horrified. She wanted to deny the accusation, but she couldn't. She never could lie. If she could, her sisters would have gotten away with a lot more of their teenage shenanigans. Janis was always the one who cracked under pressure. She was always the one who got them in trouble.

Guilt had a way of twisting confessions out of her the moment she was in the spotlight—curling around her ribs, squeezing the truth out the second someone looked her in the eye. The fact that she hadn't melted under Eunice's accusation was only due to years of navigating around her sister's particular brand of torture.

The heat of a thousand suns settled on her cheeks. "I don't have a crush on Thomas."

Her twin moaned as she rolled her head back. "You have *got* to be kidding me."

Janis shook her head but sweat was already breaking on her brow. Her throat tightened, and her chest grew heavy. "Leave it alone."

"You finally fall for a guy, and he's married to your sister?"

The words landed like a slap. Eunie was good at that. At using that condescending tone to belittle Janis.

The elevator door slid open, and Eunie shut up. Only because there was a couple inside. The pair stepped to one side to make room. Though they didn't seem to notice, the air in the small space was thick. Heavy. The tension surrounded Janis like a cocoon, wrapping her up and refusing to let her escape.

Janis was so desperate to get out of the car that she would have pushed the emergency button had it been on her side of the claustrophobic box. Unfortunately, the strangers stood between her and the ability to stop their descent.

When the elevator reached the ground floor, the gentleman smiled at her and her sister as he gestured for them to exit first. Janis mumbled her thanks as she stepped into the lobby with Eunice by her side.

They crossed the lobby, side by side, and exited through the automatic sliding doors. Fresh air greeted them, and a shiver ran through Janis. Not because she was cold, but because she was about to get lectured about her feelings for Thomas—feelings she had hidden well enough until her mom and sister started picking her apart, layer by humiliating layer.

Eunie dug in her purse as they walked, producing a cigarette and lighter moments later. Like the longtime smoker she was, she was so well practiced at igniting the tobacco that she didn't even need to stop walking. The lighter clicked as it made a small fire and a second later, the scent of her bad habit surrounded them.

After she dropped the lighter back into her purse, she draped the neon green pleather strap over her shoulder and blew out a big cloud of smoke.

"I don't blame you," she said, lacking any emotion. "He's adorable but, Janis—"

Jan rarely became angry. She spent her time being passive, disappearing, being agreeable to avoid conflict. But something clicked in her and, like the lighter, a fire started to burn.

"What do you think I'm going to do, Eunice? Steal him away from her?" The words shot out of her before she could stop them. She snorted in a completely uncharacteristic way. She wasn't a snorter. Or a confronter. Nor was she the type of woman who developed crushes.

Because it *wasn't* a crush.

Not like Eunie had assumed when she spat the word out in the hotel hallway. This wasn't some schoolgirl fantasy. She wasn't a band geek swooning over the quarterback.

Janis *loved* Thomas. Down to her bones. The kind of love that made people do stupid things, say the wrong words, and twist themselves into knots to see someone smile. The kind that made stupid women ache and hope and grieve all at once.

The kind of love destined to break her heart.

"Leave it alone," Janis warned her and picked up her pace.

She wished she'd changed her shoes. The heels she'd worn to dinner weren't high, only an inch or so, but she'd been wearing them most of the day. Her feet throbbed with every step. She preferred practical shoes. Flats with cushioning to soften the strain on her arches. As a librarian, she spent most of her days on her feet. She knew better than to wear heals. But, like the dress, she'd allowed Eunice to choose them for her.

Janis hated the shoes. She hated the dress. And more than anything, she *hated* her twin sister.

Not the casual, sibling-rivalry kind of hate. Not the annoyed sister kind of way. In the kind of way that made Janis wish she never had to see Eunice again. Ever.

Eunie drew on her cigarette again. "What are you going to tell Susan?"

Janis came to a dead stop and gawked at her. "Nothing. And neither are you."

"I have to—"

Narrowing her eyes, much like her mother had at supper, Janis glared. "No, you don't. You're being vicious. To me and to Susan. What does it matter how I feel? They're married now."

"She has a right to know."

"Why?"

A condescending smirk tugged at Eunie's lip.

Janis saw it for what it was—merriment. Her evil twin was enjoying herself. Thriving on the secret she'd uncovered. This wasn't about telling the truth or being loyal to Susan.

This was about stirring up drama. About having a power play. About throwing Janis under the bus for the sick thrill of it.

This was gossip gold. Enough to feed Eunie and her circle of friends for months.

Susan would be devastated. Thomas would be embarrassed. And Janis?

She would be mortified. Laughed at. Torn to shreds.

She could hear them now. *Stupid Janis. Naïve Janis. Homely, lonely Janis.*

That was always good for a round of chatter between Eunie and her friends.

Rage boiled in Janis's chest. She didn't understand why Eunice had to be so ruthless, but this was nothing new. She'd *always* been that way. One might think that a sister—a twin, no less—would defend the other, but Eunice was always the first in line to hurt Janis.

For their twelfth birthdays, Eunice had received a box filled with makeup and hair products. Janis had gotten books. Two weeks later, their father had died of a heart attack.

Those books had become sacred to Janis—her last tangible connection to her dad. She'd read them over and over until the pages were worn from flipping them. She'd kept them tucked away like treasures.

Until Eunie ruined them over a year later.

She swore it was an accident, that she'd never do something like that to hurt her twin. But Janis knew better. Her sister had destroyed them because Janis still had something from their father long after Eunie's lipstick and eyeshadow had run out. And Eunice could never stand it when Janis had something that she didn't.

Even though she was stronger. Prettier. More confident. Even though she walked into every room like it belonged to her.

Still, it wasn't enough.

She always had to stomp all over Janis—as if Janis could get any lower than she already was.

A grown woman, who had never known the touch of a man—yet had fallen helplessly, hopelessly in love with one she could never have. Her sister's husband.

Yes, that made for good gossip. The kind of thing people snickered about when they thought she wasn't listening. Maybe even felt a little sorry for, before brushing it off with a smug, *She's always been a little strange, hasn't she?*

But it wasn't just that.

It wasn't because she was ugly. Or unlovable. Or uninterested.

It was because connection never came easy to her. Small talk felt like a foreign language, and flirting was a skill she'd never learned. She wasn't the kind of woman who got noticed. Not in high school, not in college, not at work. She'd always felt like she was sitting outside the room where everyone else was laughing.

There had been a young man once. In her twenties. Kind, gentle, patient. He'd taken her to bookstores and coffee shops and made her believe, for a little while, that someone might actually want her for exactly who she was.

Then he'd told her he wished she would come out of her shell. That being with her was like trying to date a ghost.

It hadn't been cruel—simply honest. But it had gutted her.

After that, she stopped trying. Stopped risking. Kept her heart locked away where it could stay safe. Invisible.

Until Thomas.

Until that one Thanksgiving, when he walked into her mother's kitchen and looked at her like she *wasn't* invisible. When he smiled and asked about her favorite book, and then actually listened when she answered.

She should've known better. Should've closed the door before it ever opened.

But she hadn't. And now she was here—almost forty, completely alone, in love with a man she could never have, with her sister staring at her like she was some kind of joke.

Janis swallowed, ready to call Eunie on her malice. Tell her how unfair it was that she twisted everything into a weapon.

Before she could find her words, someone shoved Janis. *Hard.*

She stumbled forward, crashing into Eunice, who dropped her cigarette as she caught her. The smell of ash and perfume clung to her clothes.

Eunie shot her arm out to steady her, and her eyes went

wide as she looked over Janis's shoulder. Though Eunice had never been protective of her twin, she wrapped her arm around Janis and hugged her closer. "What the hell is wrong with you?" she demanded in a shrill tone.

"Give me your purse," a man demanded.

Janis's heart flipped. The voice was rough, demanding—too close. She didn't dare turn around. Her limbs locked up and her breath snagged somewhere in her throat. Her pulse pounded in her ears, drowning out everything else. She clutched her purse tighter, fingers trembling, her mind scrambling for something—*anything*—to do.

Eunice, of course, didn't miss a beat. She let out a bitter, not-on-your-life laugh. "Screw off."

Janis blinked, her mind racing to catch up. Her hands trembled as she gripped the strap of her bag. Everything seemed to be on the line, and Eunice was being defiant. As always.

The man pulled out a knife, flicked it open, and waved the blade as a devilish grin curled his lips. "Give me your fucking purse."

"Eunie," Jan whispered, her voice trembling with fear.

The thug's smirk turned condescending. "*Eunie*," he said in a mocking tone. "Give me the fucking purse, *Eunie*."

"Come get it," she dared and stepped forward, as if to prove that she wasn't intimidated.

Janis's heart sank, and the handful of bites she had forced herself to eat churned angrily in her stomach. Her sister was an idiot, she'd never doubted that, but this was reckless. Dangerous. Janis wanted to say her name again but stopped herself.

The last time hadn't gone so well.

Janis fumbled to get her purse strap off her shoulder. Maybe if he had her purse, he would leave. However, Eunie threw an arm out, stopping her.

"*Come* get *it*," the rebellious twin dared the man again.

Janis swallowed hard, fear crawling up her throat like a vine. Her hands trembled. And the man smiled—slow and satisfied—like he'd been waiting for this exact invitation.

Then he lunged.

Janis squealed as she stumbled backward. But like the hardheaded fool she was, Eunice held fast onto her bag, cussing at him, wrestling over her belongings.

The two of them spun in a chaotic blur of limbs and rage and fear.

Janis stood frozen. As always.

And then, after a loud scream, Eunie stood frozen, too. With one last yank, the guy pulled the purse from her clenched fist.

He turned toward Janis. Their eyes met.

She didn't think as she held her bag out to him, arms shaking. He snatched it from her hands and disappeared into the shadows, swallowed by the night.

Janis stared at the darkness where he'd gone, her breath catching in short, sharp bursts.

Then Eunie gripped her hand and whispered her name. This time, her voice wasn't filled with warning for Janis to do what she told her. Or mocking Janis's unrequited feelings for Thomas.

Her voice was a plea.

Eunice sounded scared.

Janis turned to her.

Eunie's eyes were wide, stunned. Her mouth moving

but silent—like her brain was still trying to catch up with her body. She looked hollow.

Janis's gaze dropped.

The stain was small at first. A bloom, no larger than a thumbprint, right over her sternum. Then it spread—slow and steady—like a dark rose opening its petals across the bright tangerine fabric.

"Oh my God," Jan whispered.

The rose kept growing, blooming wider, fuller, bolder.

When Eunie stumbled, Jan caught her. Helped her down onto the sidewalk as gently as she could. Her knees hit the concrete, but she didn't feel the sting.

She reached out, brushing a tear from the corner of Eunie's eye with the back of her knuckle.

"It's okay, Eunie. It's okay," she said, her voice softer than she expected. There was an eerie calm taking root in her—like the world had narrowed to this one moment, and everything else had gone silent. She stared at the flower blooming across her sister's chest.

"Jan," Eunice wheezed. "Call for help."

Janis nodded and reached for her purse before recalling she'd surrendered it. She looked back to the hotel. There had been a security guard wandering the lobby when they'd left. The sign for the hotel was several blocks away. She hadn't realized how far they'd walked.

Janis glanced around for someone to call. Looking one way, then the other, she saw no one. Not even the jerk who'd mugged them.

Leaning over her, she started to tell Eunie to hang on. To wait. She'd be right back.

But then she recalled why they were there. Why they'd

taken this walk. More than that, she recalled the sneer on Eunie's face as she'd said she had no intention of keeping Janis's secret.

She was going to tell Susan.

She was going to tell *Thomas*.

And once she did, Jan would probably never see him again.

He'd disappear from her life. She'd never hear his gentle voice again. He'd never laugh at one of her lame jokes.

She couldn't let that happen. She *wouldn't*.

"Jan," Eunice whispered.

Janis leaned over her.

"Get help." She was getting weaker.

"I can't." Janis leaned even closer. "I can't leave you." She tried to be comforting, sympathetic even, but she heard how cold her voice was. How detached she sounded. Like someone else was speaking through her.

She stared at the open wound in her sister's chest. The torn front of her shirt was now soaked with blood. Janis rested her palm on the glistening wound, but she couldn't find the strength to press. Couldn't summon the will to try to stop the bleeding.

As thick, velvety liquid covered her hand, oozing between her fingers, Janis's mind dragged her backward.

Ninth grade.

Science class.

She'd started her period without warning, causing a dark stain on the back of her khakis. She'd gone to the nurse who had summoned for Eunice, hoping Janis's twin had a spare pair of pants. Instead of sympathizing with her twin, Eunice had told friends and word spread through the entire school. By the end of the day, Janis's new nickname was *Bloody Mary*. People whispered it in the halls. Laughed behind her back. For *months*.

Janis blinked back to the present, her hand still slick with blood, her sister staring up at her—scared, vulnerable, silent.

A part of Janis wanted to scream. To run for help. To pretend none of this was happening.

But another part—the one still bleeding from ninth grade, from a thousand cuts just like it—stayed frozen. The part of her that was madly in love with Thomas refused to let her move.

"Help," Eunie whispered.

But the memory clung to her skin like the blood still slicking her hand—raw, undeniable. And not only that memory. *All* the memories. All the times Eunice had made her feel small, invisible, stupid. The taunts, the smirks, the betrayal.

As Janis looked into her sister's eyes, the truth settled in her chest like stone.

If she saved her—if she called for help and kept her alive—Eunie would ruin her. Like always. Only this time, it wouldn't be whispered names in school hallways. It wouldn't be humiliation.

She was going to take Thomas away.

Janis couldn't let that happen. She might not have Thomas, but he was in her life. Close to her. He was here to see her. Talk to her. She could imagine he was hers—but not if Eunice turned him against her.

Instead of calling for help, Jan started to stroke Eunie's hair but stopped when she realized her fingers were covered in blood. But then she smirked as a strange sense of satisfaction came over her.

She ran her hand over Eunie's hair. *Bloody Mary.*

"You're wrong," she whispered. "I don't have a crush on Thomas. It's more than that."

"Jan," she said again, barely loud enough to be heard. "Please."

"I love him, Eunie." She continued brushing her hand over Eunice's hair, like she'd done hundreds of times when her older sister was sick or upset. "I love him like I've never loved anyone. Like I could never love anyone again."

"Jan," Eunie whispered again.

"I'm sorry. But I won't let you take him away from me. Not *ever.*"

Fear filled Eunie's eyes. Maybe even a little bit of understanding. The mocking was gone. The control. Everything that had always made her *Eunie.*

She stared at Janis.

Gasped.

And then she stopped breathing.

Chapter Three

Within minutes of Eunie's last breath, someone kneeled beside Janis. She numbly explained that she and her sister had been mugged. After that, everything blurred—sirens, voices, motion. She couldn't track the order of events, only the weight of her limbs and the ringing in her ears.

Soon after the police arrived, Janis was taken to the station—a squat, square building with faded peach walls and dusty windows. The inside smelled faintly of bleach, old coffee, and sweat. A ceiling fan spun overhead but did nothing to ease the humidity clinging to her skin.

Someone scraped dried blood from her hands and nails, and then she was told to wash the remaining blood from her hands and change from her too yellow dress with the blood stains into an itchy pair of dark blue scrubs that sounded like sheets of paper sliding around every time she moved. They were stiff and too large. The rough fabric made her skin feel raw. The neck sagged. The elastic waistband barely held. She looked like a patient, or worse—a prisoner.

A uniformed officer with tired eyes and deep creases around his mouth escorted her down a long, echoing corridor. The paper booties on her feet made shuffling sounds as she did her best to not slide.

Fluorescent lights flickered overhead. Doors lined both sides of the hallway, some open to cluttered offices, others closed and silent. The walls were painted a dull off-white that had yellowed with age.

At the end of the hall, he opened a metal door and led her into a cold room with concrete walls, a battered table, and two mismatched folding chairs. A camera sat mounted in the corner like an unblinking eye.

The feet of the chair scraped over the cracked linoleum floor as he slid it out and gestured for her to sit. He gave her a cup of water, and then a female officer started asking her questions in a soothing but heavily accented voice.

What did the man look like?

What did he say?

What was in her purse?

Janis was numb as she answered automatically, staring past her at the yellowed wall, barely hearing the words coming out of her own mouth. She had tried to make eye contact, fearing she'd look guilty if she didn't, but her social awkwardness—or perhaps her shame at what she'd done—wouldn't allow her. Staring at the wall was easier. Less terrifying. Less guilt-inducing.

She had no idea how long she'd been there before her eyes started to feel like someone had dumped sand in them. Her shoulders began to stoop, and things started to become foggy. Finally, the door to the small room opened and a man stepped inside speaking Spanish. While she understood the basics of the language, she had to take time to process and translate the words. She couldn't do that with how quickly the other man was talking.

The woman who had been questioning her turned to Janis. "We found security footage of the incident, Ms. Duke. We have him on video."

The way the man exhaled—his body language loosening slightly—made it clear they'd been waiting for her to crack. Waiting for her to confess. To say she'd killed her sister.

The thought crawled across her skin like ice. Had she killed her sister? Was letting her bleed to death murder?

The questions circled her mind like vultures, slow and deliberate, waiting for her to admit the truth. To herself. To anyone.

She hadn't stabbed Eunice. She hadn't touched the knife. But she hadn't helped, either.

And wasn't that, in some small, quiet way the same thing?

"Take her back to the hotel," the man who had interrupted her questioning said in English. He finally focused on Janis. "I assure you. We will find the man who did this."

She thought she smiled. Or tried to. But her face didn't quite cooperate. Her lips twitched. Her jaw ached. She wasn't sure if it showed. Wasn't sure she cared.

When the police brought her back to the hotel, they were met by the nervous hotel manager waiting inside the lobby. He smoothed his hands down the front of his blazer and glanced uneasily at the officers flanking her.

"Señorita, I am very sorry," he said, his voice laced with worry. "Please, anything you need—tea, coffee, food—we will bring it to your room. No charge."

His gaze darted between Janis and the officers, and he offered another stiff smile, the kind used to soothe guests *and* avoid conflict.

She understood his anxiety. A violent incident involving guests—even if it had happened outside hotel grounds—could reflect badly on the establishment. Bad press. Bad reviews. Nervous travelers might cancel reservations. The presence of uniformed police alone could send the wrong message to anyone walking through the lobby.

She managed a small shake of her head. "No, thank you."

Her stomach churned with nausea from the weight of the night. Tea wouldn't help. Nothing would.

They were silent as they rode the elevator to the third floor.

Right before the doors opened, the officer beside her spoke in a low, careful voice. "Would you prefer to tell them yourself," he asked, "or would you like me to?"

Janis blinked at him. Her mind needed a few seconds to process the words. The thought of speaking—of saying out loud that Eunice was dead—felt impossible.

But so did the idea of someone else having that moment. Losing Eunice would be her mother's undoing. The grief would split her open. Eunie was the favorite, the golden child, the daughter who could do no wrong. The center of Phylis's universe.

Janis had spent a lifetime watching that bond from the outside, like a kid pressing her face to the glass of someone else's home.

Now, she'd be the one to shatter it.

And somewhere deep inside—somewhere quiet and dark—she was glad.

Glad it would be *her* voice that broke the news. Glad it would be *her* words that changed everything. Her mother would never forget this moment, and it would come with *Janis's* face attached. She felt the twitch of something unfamiliar in her chest. Not pride. Not exactly.

Satisfaction.

"I'll do it."

The doors slid open with a soft chime.

Once they reached the hotel room the Dukes had been sharing, the manager pulled out a master key and unlocked the door.

"Perhaps we shouldn't wake her. Mom doesn't like being disturbed," she whispered before he could open the door.

The manager placed his hand on her arm. "The officer had some questions for her. Remember?"

"Right." Janis supposed the other people entering the room with her thought she wasn't looking forward to telling her mother what happened. And maybe she *should* have been. But a small, shameful part of her was eager.

Not to speak the words. Not to relive those last moments with Eunie. But to *see* the anguish on her mother's face. To watch the heartbreak settle over the woman who had never once shown her an ounce of compassion. The woman who had only ever truly grieved when something happened to *Eunie*.

The only time Eunie had been forced to do anything—like make Janis her bridesmaid—was when Phylis was concerned what other people would think. If Janis hadn't been in Eunice's bridal party, people would have talked. They would have questioned what kind of family the Dukes were. They would have thought less of Phylis, and she couldn't—*wouldn't*—allow that.

Reminding herself that smiling at her mother's pain was not the correct response—no matter how satisfying it might feel—Janis took a deep breath and stepped inside.

Disappointment washed over her like cold water.

Her mother wasn't sleeping. She was standing between Susan and Thomas.

"Where the hell have you two been?" Phylis spun toward Janis as fury filled her face. "I woke up and you weren't back and . . ." Her lecture faded to silence as she seemed to finally notice Eunice was missing. Her eyes flicked to the uniformed police officer beside Janis. She clutched the front of her robe tighter, her bravado wilting in an instant. "What . . . What's going on?" she asked, her voice uncharacteristically thin.

Thomas put his hand on Phylis's shoulder. His usual easy confidence was replaced with quiet unease. Susan's expression had begun to shift, too. Her face sank from concern to confusion as she took in Janis's appearance. "Janis?" Susan asked. "Why are you dressed like that?" The air in the room grew thick as the three of them scanned over the scrubs. "Where's Eunice?"

Silence followed. Heavy and brittle.

Janis opened her mouth, but no sound came out. She didn't have to answer. She watched fear wash over them—first in Susan's face, the subtle widening of her eyes, the way her lips parted as if forming a silent no. Then in Phylis's posture, stiffening like she'd been slapped, her mouth snapping shut.

They didn't need Janis to say it. They already knew.

Something terrible had happened.

Phylis opened her mouth but no words came. Her

face—usually so sharp, so sure—wavered. The color drained from her cheeks. Her chin quivered. And then, in a voice hoarse and barely audible, she asked, "Where's Eunie?"

The fear in her eyes was new. Strange. Beautiful, in a twisted sort of way.

Janis had never seen it before. She'd seen rage, disappointment, disdain—but not this. Not uncertainty. Not helplessness. And for one breathless moment, she relished it. The way her mother's iron spine seemed to wilt under the weight of something she couldn't control. Couldn't fix. Couldn't dress up for the neighbors.

Dead.

Simply thinking the word brought an unsettling sense of peace to Janis.

The room had gone still, but inside her chest something fluttered. Not grief. Not relief. Something quieter. Darker. *Lighter.*

A part of her—some quiet, buried part that had spent its whole life being ignored—whispered, *"This is what it feels like to be seen."*

Phylis was finally looking at her. Looking at her with fear in her eyes.

And Janis wasn't sure she wanted that to stop.

Her lips twitched—not into a smile, but she feared she wouldn't be able to stop them, so she lowered her face and, despite having scrubbed her hands at the police station, she saw them covered in red.

Blood. *Eunice's* blood.

"We were mugged." Unlike her mother, Janis's voice sounded remarkably calm. "Eunie tried to fight him."

"Where is she?" Susan asked again.

"Answer us," their mother squawked in a high-pitched, ear-piercing voice. Her dramatic voice. The show was about to begin. This time her hysterics were warranted, but Janis had been exposed to her over-the-top reactions for years.

She barely flinched. She knew that voice. The *performance* voice. The one Phylis used when she wanted attention or sympathy—or control. This time, maybe the hysteria was warranted, but that didn't make it any easier to stomach. Janis had grown tired of her mother's dramatics years ago, like someone tuning out a show they'd already seen too many times.

Susan rushed to Janis and gripped her hands. "Jan? Jan, please. What's going on?"

When Janis lifted her face, her gaze landed on Thomas. He looked even more sun-kissed than he had at the wedding. His tanned olive skin made him look like a movie star. The same sense of shame she always felt when she thought of Thomas washed over her. She looked at her hands again.

They were clean. She'd scrubbed them at the police station until her knuckles were raw. But now, in the low hotel lighting, she swore she saw red. Bright at first, then darkening—seeping into her skin. Filling the creases of her palms. Pooling beneath her short fingernails.

She wondered if she would always see them that way now.

"Janis," Phylis demanded, "where is your sister?"

The accusation in her voice was enough to cause Janis to face her again. A sense of pleasure settled over her heart, and she reminded herself to keep her voice even as she spoke so as to not reveal her true feelings. "We were

-mugged," she said again. "Eunie tried to fight back."

Susan gripped Jan's hands harder.

"He stabbed her," Janis said.

Phylis cried out. And there it was. The overly dramatic reaction from her mother. "Where's my Eunie? Where is she?"

"Jan?" Susan asked more calmly. Her face had lost all color, and her blue eyes widened, but her voice remained steady. "Where's Eunie?"

"He killed her," Janis said, looking at her mother as she did.

When Susan swayed on her feet, Thomas rushed toward them. He turned Susan into his arms and hugged her closely as she cried.

"Were you hurt?" he asked Janis. The first to show any concern for her wellbeing.

"No."

Relief washed over his face. His caring nature shone through. "Good. That's good."

As Susan pulled from Thomas and embraced her sister, Janis watched their mother's hysterics kick into high gear. She wailed until Thomas left the sisters and attempted to calm his new mother-in-law. Phylis screamed, cried, and threw herself onto the bed like a child having a tantrum. That's what she looked like, too. A toddler who hadn't gotten her way. That's how she always looked when she acted like this.

Susan ran her hand over Janis's hair. "If you weren't hurt, why are you dressed like this?"

Turning her focus to the paper scrubs, Janis frowned. "They took my clothes."

"The muggers?" Susan asked with horror.

"The police."

Susan turned an accusing glare at the officer standing behind them. "Why would you do that? After what she went through?"

The police officer stepped forward. "Ms. Duke's clothing could potentially be evidence in the case."

"I tried to . . ." Janis's voice faded as she relived the moment when the life seeped out of Eunice. She had to take a moment to breathe so she didn't show her true feelings. "She was bleeding. A lot."

Her mother screamed out—sharp and ragged. The kind of desperate sound that didn't simply fill the room but *shook* it.

Janis felt it in her bones. In her teeth.

And for the first time ever, she savored the sound of her mother's screams. The rawness. The helplessness. The sound of her mother's cruelty breaking.

"I tried to help. There was so much blood. I couldn't stop it. I tried."

Susan pulled Janis into another tight hug. "I know you did," she whispered. "I know you did, Jan."

The manager, who had been standing by, stepped forward. "We are so sorry for your loss. The resort has a resident physician on call. Should I see if we can give Mrs. Duke something to calm her?"

"Yes, please," Thomas said.

The sound of the door closing indicated that the manager had left their room. Janis assumed the police officer had left as well, until he said, "I need to ask your mother a few questions."

Janis didn't have a chance to say anything before Thomas stepped in. "I'll stay with Phylis. Susan, you should help Janis change."

Janis looked at herself in the mirror while Susan opened the suitcase that sat on the stand next to the dresser.

Her reflection startled her—eyes glassy, face pale, lips dry and lifeless. The shapeless scrubs clung awkwardly to her body.

She barely recognized herself.

And yet something in her expression tugged at her. Something in the tightness around her mouth, the flicker of something behind her eyes.

Was she smiling?

Not fully. Not quite. But there was a tension there. Like a smile threatening to rise. Like the truth of what she'd done—*what she'd allowed*—was pulling at the corners of her lips.

She dropped her gaze before it could reach the surface.

Susan handed her some clothes, and they walked to the restroom in silence.

Once they were alone, Susan let out a sob. "I'm so sorry, Jan. I'm so sorry. If we hadn't brought you all to Mexico—"

Janis shook her head. "She refused to give him her purse. She taunted him." Her voice was flat. Matter of fact. Emotionless. "You know how she is," she added but then caught her mistake. "*Was*."

Susan winced but didn't argue. Her eyes searched Janis's face for something she couldn't name.

After a moment, she said gently, "Can you tell me what happened?"

Janis hesitated. Her throat tightened. The memory was already there—pressed like a handprint in her mind.

"We were walking. Talking . . . Arguing, really. She lit a cigarette and wouldn't stop pushing. Picking. Taunting. She was enjoying herself. And then—" Janis swallowed hard. "He came out of nowhere. One second, it was only us and the street. The next . . ."

She blinked. Her eyes burned. The back of her neck prickled. "He shoved me first. Hard. I nearly fell. Then he pulled out a knife and told us to give him our purses." Her voice dropped to a whisper. "She dared him to take them."

Susan's eyes widened. "Oh, God."

"She said, 'Come get it.' Like it was a joke." Janis paused, pressing her palms into her thighs to ground herself. "He lunged. They fought. She wouldn't let go of her bag. I-I couldn't move."

The image of Eunice gasping, the blood soaking through her shirt, the sudden stillness—it all came rushing back.

Janis blinked as her eyes started to burn. She felt tears fill them like acid but she didn't think the tears were due to sadness. Her eyes were dry from the long night. But she let the tears form and drip down her cheeks. She'd learned the value of good theatrics from her mother. "It happened so fast."

Susan covered her mouth with her hand, her face pale as tears slipped down her cheeks.

"I tried to stop the bleeding," Janis added, though her voice lacked conviction. "There was so much blood."

For a moment it looked like Susan might cry again. She reached out—started to open her arms—but stopped halfway, her hands hanging awkwardly in the air between them. She started to open her arms but stopped.

Janis didn't move.

Susan let her arms drop, her face crumpling once more. She wiped beneath her eyes with the heel of her hand and gave a shaky laugh that didn't quite land.

"She could be so mean sometimes," she said quietly, almost like a confession. "I loved her, but God, she could be *so* mean."

Janis didn't say anything. She didn't have to.

"Do you remember when she convinced Danny Umbridge to dump me?" Susan's voice was thin, almost embarrassed. "She said he was too good for me—that he'd break my heart eventually, so it was better to get it over with." She gave a short, humorless laugh. "Maybe she was right. But God, she was so *heartless* about it." Susan sighed. "Even so, she didn't deserve *this*. No one does."

Silence settled between them, heavy and uneven.

Then Susan suddenly gasped. "Oh God—Roger. Someone needs to call Roger." She turned, frantic now. "And the kids. The *kids*, Jan. They've lost their mom."

Janis's stomach twisted. She felt it immediately—like a knot tightening deep in her gut.

The kids.

Not Eunie. Not her sister. Not the one who had humiliated her, ignored her, overshadowed her. But Lily and Caleb. Her niece and nephew.

She loved them. She always had.

And they were going to grow up without their mother now.

Grief exploded in her chest—not for Eunie, but for *them*. For what they'd lost. For what they'd never understand.

Janis remembered what it felt like to lose *her* person. Her father. The only one who had ever made her feel truly seen. Truly loved. While Eunie had been a carbon copy of Phylis, Jan was exactly like her dad. Their quiet nature, love of reading, and a softness that others saw as weakness.

She had been twelve, still trying to figure out how to fit into a world that didn't seem to want her. And then he was gone. A sudden, gaping hole where safety used to be.

She remembered how loud the silence was after. How nothing tasted right for months. How everyone expected her to get over it, especially Phylis. Especially Eunie.

Now Lily and Caleb would have to carry that same ache. Something tightened in her throat. *They didn't deserve that.* None of this was their fault.

Her lips parted, but no words came out. Instead, she simply nodded.

Susan gave her a soft touch on the shoulder—brief, uncertain. "Let's get you out of those clothes," she said. "A shower will do you good."

She started the water while Janis stepped out of the rough material and wrapped a towel around herself. Susan carefully bundled it up and put it into the trashcan. She sniffled again, staring at the scrubs before easing the trashcan down. As tears slid down her cheeks, she slid the shower curtain open for Janis.

"Do you want me to stay?" Susan asked.

Jan shook her head. "No. Check on Mom. I'll be out soon."

"Okay." Susan hesitated. "I'm really glad you weren't hurt." Then she left.

Steam rose, curling around the light above the mirror, fogging the glass. Janis stood still for a moment, watching her reflection disappear into gray.

Maybe that was better. Maybe she didn't need to see

herself right now. Not like this. Emotionless. Cold. Detached.

Janis slipped off the towel—stiff from too much bleach during the laundering process—and stepped into the water. The steady stream was too hot, but she didn't adjust the knobs.

The pain felt like penance. Like punishment. Like a secret she couldn't scrub off.

She closed her eyes, let the water pound against her shoulders, and tried to steady her breathing. But her mind wouldn't still. She kept replaying the moment—not the violence, not Eunice falling—but the *pause* right before deciding to let her sister die.

The breath she took. The decision she made. She could've screamed louder. Run faster. Pressed harder on the wound. Tried more. She hadn't.

She let it happen. And now it was done.

Closing her eyes, Janis let the water soak her hair. There was something hovering outside the edges of her awareness, something that hadn't caught up to her yet.

What if the police dug deeper? What if there was more footage? What if someone saw something she didn't know about? What if Susan started to really look at her? What if *Thomas* did?

Janis's stomach twisted. She'd told herself she did nothing wrong. That she froze. That it was too late. But she hadn't *frozen*. She'd *chosen*.

And now, she didn't know who—or *what*—that made her.

She stood under the hot water as the peace she found in Eunice's departure started to turn to fear. She couldn't quite believe what she'd done. But it was done. And she'd done it.

Finally, she couldn't stand the heat any longer. She felt lightheaded and found breathing increasingly difficult. She turned off the water and dried skin that had turned crimson from the heat. She wrapped her hair in a towel and dressed in the shirt and knee-length shorts Susan had set out for her.

When she left the bathroom, a different man was standing next to their mother speaking with Thomas and Susan as the police officer stood by.

When Thomas noticed her, he said, "This is Dr. Hernandez. He's the resort physician."

"I'd like to give your mother a sedative. Do you know of any allergies or medications?"

Janis gestured toward the pills by the bed. "Those are hers. That's all she's taking. She doesn't have any allergies."

Janis had barely gotten the words out before her mother started crying again. Her shoulders trembled, but this time, no sound came. No dramatic wails. No gasps for attention. Just a quiet, guttural kind of grief. She covered her face with her hands. Her body folded in on itself, smaller than Janis had ever seen her. Fragile. Real.

And that was the part Janis couldn't quite process.

Because this wasn't Phylis putting on a show. This wasn't her mother's usual theatrics—loud enough for the neighbors, timed perfectly for sympathy. This was real. But that only made Janis even more angry. Watching her mother fall apart didn't evoke sympathy. It stirred up something bitter deep inside.

She hadn't even asked how Janis was after watching her sister die. She hadn't been glad that Janis had survived. Hadn't even noticed, really. Had Phylis Duke ever cared about *anyone* other than Eunice?

Seconds later, the doctor injected the woman with a needle and talked to her in a soft, reassuring tone. By the time he walked around the bed, Phylis had started to calm down. Thomas stood by her, patting her hand, until she finally fell asleep.

"Thank God," Janis whispered, not meaning to.

The doctor stopped in front of her. "Janis, may I examine you?"

"I wasn't hurt," she said.

He smiled sweetly at her. His reddish-tan skin was smooth except for the slight wrinkles at the corners of his eyes when he smiled at her. "Sometimes, when we experience a trauma, we don't realize we've been injured."

"Let him have a look at you, Jan," Susan said. "Please."

Janis nodded, and he turned to his bag.

"Let me check your pupils." He stepped forward and shone a light in her eyes. And then he checked her blood pressure. He looked at her hands and arms, turned them over, and then bent to check her legs. "May I lift your shirt to check your torso?"

Janis darted her gaze at Susan who nodded. She then looked at Thomas. He turned around—deliberate, careful, as if to give her privacy. And that was when the shame crept in. Not because Thomas wasn't looking. But because someone else *was*. Even if it was a doctor. Even if it meant nothing. In her mind, the only man who had ever seen her—truly seen her—had been Thomas. In her mind, he was the only one allowed to look.

But that was fantasy. And this was real.

Her skin prickled at the feeling of betrayal. Like disloyalty to a love that was never hers to begin with. With no way to refuse without seeming temperamental, Janis stood so the doctor could examine her.

The doctor made quick work of checking her for injuries. He suggested she sit again, so she did. "Did you sleep at all last night?"

"No. I was with the police."

"Would you like something to help you relax?"

Again, she looked at Susan.

She nodded. "Let's make sure you get some rest, okay?"

"Okay." Janis watched as the doctor stuck a needle into her skin. The sensation of warmth hit her as the fluid went into her vein and started to spread quickly through her body.

Susan helped her stand, steadying her with gentle hands. "Would it be okay if you slept in the bed next to Mom?" she asked. "Thomas and I can take the other one, in case you or she need anything."

Janis nodded, too tired to protest. Too ashamed to admit the way her stomach twisted at the thought.

She had no right to feel anything. Not after everything that had happened. But still—knowing he'd be lying in bed beside Susan, so close, while she lay beside Phylis . . . made her feel smaller than ever.

She let Susan guide her to the edge of the bed, the one where her mother was already asleep, and eased her under the covers.

After brushing a hand over Janis's hair, Susan spoke sweetly, as if comforting a young child. "I'll be right here if you need anything. I'm not going anywhere."

"Okay," Janis said.

She closed her eyes and listened to the whispered voices.

"She's so calm," Susan said in a hushed tone.

"She's in shock but that will wear off," the doctor said. "You'll want to keep an eye on her. If you get concerned about either of them, call the front desk. I'll be close by."

"Thank you," Thomas said.

"When can we go home?" Susan asked.

Jan opened her eyes enough to see the police officer standing with Susan and Thomas.

There was a stretch of silence before the man with the heavy accent answered. "Not until after your sister's autopsy has been completed and the coroner releases her body."

A muffled cry came from Susan.

"Someone will be in touch with you to let you know," the officer said.

"Thank you," Thomas said.

Moments later, the door clicked, and Susan let out another soft sob. Janis forced her heavy lids open in time to see Thomas hug her close to him and kiss her head.

Though it hadn't been her plan, Janis couldn't say that she was sorry their honeymoon had been interrupted.

Chapter Four

The sky outside the window was tinted with shades of pink and orange when Janis awoke. As she opened her eyes, she was met with the sight of two sleeping bodies in the bed next to where she'd fallen asleep beside her mother.

Thomas snored softly, and she nearly laughed. The happy moment didn't last long, however. He was in bed with Susan. His wife. Janis's sister. Rolling to her other side, determined to stop feeling her heart race at the sight of Thomas sleeping, Janis was met with her mother's pale face. Drool ran from the corner of her mouth as she breathed, deep and slow.

The forbidden love in Janis's heart instantly turned to revulsion.

The grin that had tugged at her lips a few moments before turned into a scowl. While Thomas's sweet snores had sounded endearing, hearing her mother's wheezing inhales made Janis want to choke her.

Closing her eyes, she tried to block out the angry feelings, but they grew with each obnoxious inhale she had to endure.

As a child, Janis remembered lying awake while Phylis napped on the sofa during her sacred "rest time," insisting on complete silence throughout the house. No, the children couldn't go outside—there'd be no one to supervise them. And *no*, Jan couldn't go to her room—she had to stay in the living room, stationed like a sentinel in case someone called or rang the bell. Someone had to intercept the noise before it reached their mother's delicate ears.

Janis would try to read, pretending not to hear the thick, wet breathing coming from the couch beside her. But she heard it. She always heard it.

The sound of someone who took up too much space. Who demanded too much.

Who had always made her feel like a burden. And now, all these years later, that same sound still pressed down on her like a weight.

Closing her eyes, she tried to will the angry thoughts away.

But they multiplied with each rattling inhale.

Tossing the blankets off her legs, she sat, put her feet to the floor, and took several calming breaths. She had always resented her mother, but what she was feeling now was too akin to hatred.

She didn't hate her mother. Did she? Could she?

The question pulsed in her mind like a bruise pressed too hard. But something in her—a dark, twisted little voice she didn't want to name—whispered that maybe she could. Maybe she already did. Maybe she *always had*.

The feeling hadn't started with the breathing. Hadn't even started with unfair responsibilities laid upon her as the "lesser" twin. That shadow of hatred had been there all along, coiled deep inside her like a seed planted long ago. Neglect watered it. Comparison fed it. Silence, obedience, and always being the lesser one had made it grow.

She remembered being thirteen years old and winning a blue ribbon in the school spelling bee. She'd rushed home, heart soaring, clutching the thin satin ribbon in both hands.

Phylis had barely glanced at it. "Don't brag," she'd said. "No one likes a show-off."

That was it. No hug. No praise. No refrigerator display.

Her father would have been so proud, but her mother couldn't be bothered to even look at her.

Janis had stood in the hallway, that ribbon fluttering in her grip like a thing dying in the wind. The feeling she'd swallowed then—that burning, shame-filled ache—was back now.

Except this time, it didn't shrink inside her. This time, it expanded. Like the bloodstain on Eunice's shirt. Dark. Spreading. Inevitable.

She didn't want to feel this way. But she did. And the more she tried to tell herself she *didn't* hate her mother, the more she wasn't sure.

"Jan?" Susan asked.

Janis opened her eyes to see her sister sitting up, looking at her with concern. Janis forced her face to relax. "I'm sorry if I woke you."

"Are you okay?"

She wasn't sure how she was supposed to answer that. "Um. Bad dream," she lied.

"Want to talk about it?"

She shook her head. "I'm hungry. I think I'll go down to the restaurant."

A touch of panic flashed across Susan's face. "Well . . . you shouldn't go alone. I'll go with you."

Janis blinked a few times. "What about Mom?"

"Thomas can stay."

The words sent a ripple of unease through her. Janis didn't trust her mother. Not with him. Not with anyone, really—but especially not with him. Phylis had a way of twisting things, embedding doubt where none existed. She'd already accused Janis of not liking Thomas—how long before she took it further? Asked questions. Made him uncomfortable. Or worse, made *herself* out to be the wounded mother who didn't understand why her daughter was so cold and ungrateful.

Thomas was polite. Gentle. He'd never push back. He'd listen to Phylis, nod sympathetically, maybe even agree to be kind. The thought of her mother weaving her version of the truth into his ear while Susan and Janis were gone made Janis's skin crawl.

"He'll take care of her," Susan said with a reassuring tone. Clearly, she misread Janis's hesitation.

"I know. But he shouldn't have to. Maybe we should order room service."

Susan's sweet smile returned. "That sounds perfect."

Janis crossed the room to the desk and grabbed the portfolio that had the menu and a long list of tourist attractions in the area. "I'll have fruit, wheat toast, and coffee," she said, handing it to Susan without looking. She had veered from her usual the night before at dinner and had regretted it. She wasn't going to make that mistake again.

"It's almost dinner time. You slept most of the day," Susan said, but then quickly added. "But I'm sure I can get fruit and toast."

"Maybe chamomile tea would be better than coffee."

"Probably," Susan said.

After handing the portfolio to her sister, Janis grabbed some clean clothes from her suitcase and disappeared into the bathroom.

She flicked on the light and stood in front of the mirror, blinking against the brightness.

Her reflection told her she hadn't slept as well as she should have, considering the doctor had injected her with a sedative. Her skin was pale and blotchy, her eyes ringed with shadows, her lips dry and colorless. She looked hollow. Off.

She kept dreaming about Eunie's death—again and again, the same scene, the same blood. Sometimes she screamed. Sometimes she stood and watched. Sometimes she laughed.

She splashed cold water on her face, but it didn't help. Nothing felt real. She leaned closer to the mirror and studied herself. She thought she'd look different.

Being a twin without a twin had always seemed impossible. Abstract. Like a math problem with no solution. But now, here she was. Just one. On her own.

And yet her face looked exactly the same.

That was the strangest part. How normal she looked. For most of her life, being a twin had been an identity. A role. A tether. And now, that other half of her was gone—and instead of feeling freer, she felt . . . disoriented. *Lopsided*.

She touched her cheek, as if expecting to feel the shift

physically.

But the reflection didn't flinch. She stared back at herself with the same face she'd always had.

She turned away from the glass and reached for her clothes, swallowing down the familiar ache that had begun to settle like a stone in her chest.

The relief she'd felt in those first few hours—the quiet, dizzying sense of freedom that had crept in when no one was looking—was now turning bitter in her mouth. It hadn't lasted.

It couldn't.

Because now she was left with this cold, rising guilt that maybe the worst thing she'd ever done wasn't letting her sister die. It was feeling *grateful* that she had.

The police had told her there were security cameras in the area. What if one of them caught her? What if they watched the video and saw that she did nothing to help her sister? Wouldn't they arrest her? Send her to jail in Mexico?

Janis didn't know much about the country, but she assumed Americans who ended up in Mexican jails didn't fare well. The food. The overcrowding. The language barrier. The fear. It all clawed at her from the inside.

But then she played the evening over in her mind again. She had leaned over, rested her hand on Eunie's chest, stroked her hair, and when she'd spoken to her, it had barely been above a whisper. The only way anyone could possibly know what she'd done was if they'd been able to read her lips or pick up the muted conversation.

She didn't know if either of those were possible.

She didn't think they were, but she couldn't ask. Not without sounding suspicious.

Her anxiety ballooned with every passing second,

pressing hard against her chest. Instead of the steam from a warm, calming shower, she imagined the moldy scent of a communal prison bathroom, the rusted pipes, the sting of soap in her eyes. She imagined the cold floor beneath her bare feet. The sneers. The fights.

The bullying she'd endured from Eunice would be nothing compared to what she'd face in prison. There'd be no Susan to help her shoulder the bullying. No Thomas to whisper words of understanding. Just iron bars and people who didn't know who she used to be.

And worst of all, her mother would *finally* have something to be proud of: a tragedy to milk, a story to tell. She'd mourn Eunice in public, but in private she'd repeat, with a smug nod, that Janis had always been *a little off*.

By the time she finished dressing and drying her hair, Janis's chest was tight, her fingers trembling. She stared at her reflection, wide-eyed, pale, unfamiliar. Should she run?

It wasn't too late.

She could disappear. Change her name. Slip into another country and vanish. Maybe South America. She'd always wanted to see Chile—the mountains, the coast, the wild freedom of it. Maybe there, no one would know what she'd done.

Maybe if she was on the run, living someone else's life, she could finally shed the skin she'd always been forced to wear. The shell of the obedient daughter. The forgettable sister. The quiet twin.

Maybe without Eunice's shadow stretching over her, she could finally see what she looked like in sunlight.

And best of all—if she vanished now, *no one* would ever know how desperately, pathetically in love she'd been with her sister's husband.

That secret, at least, could die with her old life.

A soft knock on the bathroom door distracted her. "Yes?" she called out in a hoarse voice.

"Jan," Susan said, "dinner is here."

Janis stared at her reflection for several seconds before finally opening the door and stepping out of the shower-induced humidity. The air in the room was cooler, calmer. Her heart still raced, the remnants of her imagined escape clinging to her like steam on her skin.

Then Thomas looked up. He met her eyes.

And the panic in her chest loosened enough for her to breathe again.

He was still rumpled from sleep—his shirt wrinkled, his dark hair sticking out in a hundred directions—but he was here. Present. Close enough to touch.

He turned his attention back to the room service tray, lifting the lids from the plates that had been delivered while she was in the bathroom.

Janis stood frozen for a moment, watching him. She couldn't go.

The fantasy of fleeing to South America, of shedding her name, her life, her guilt—it all dimmed beneath the weight of this one truth: she couldn't imagine her life without him in it.

Even though she should. Even though she *knew* she should.

She had to divert her gaze so she didn't turn into a puddle at his feet. She had no idea how long they were going to have to stay in Mexico. Days? Weeks? However long it was, she suspected Thomas would be this close until they were able to return to Kansas. She wasn't sure how she would hide her feelings when he was right there. If Eunie could figure out her darkest secret, so could Susan.

"You do realize there is only one bathroom, don't you?" her mother snapped from behind her.

Janis stiffened, and years of training kicked in. She turned and forced herself to give her mother a weak smile—the kind she'd practiced her whole life to keep the peace, to stay pleasant, to avoid becoming a target. "Sorry."

Her mother muttered under her breath as she shuffled toward the bathroom.

Susan rushed to Janis. "Ignore her. She's out of sorts. We all are." Guiding Jan toward the balcony, she helped her sit. "I'll grab your food."

Moments later, Thomas carried a plate and pot of tea to the table. He set both in front of Janis. "This looks pretty good for toast and fruit."

Her heart lightened at his kind gesture. He had a way of grounding her. Of bringing her out of the darkness that always seemed to surround her. "The chef would have to try pretty hard to mess this up."

"Don't underestimate the skillset of a bad cook," he said with a wink before disappearing inside.

And there it was again. The trembling that shook her heart every time he was too kind to her. Smiled too bright. Accidentally touched her hand. Janis took a breath to calm her heart.

Susan eased into the chair next to Janis. "Everything okay?"

"Yes."

Covering Jan's hand with her own, Susan nearly pleaded with her eyes. "It's okay if you're having a hard time. You don't have to lie to protect me, Jan. We aren't kids anymore. I know you're hurt, too."

"I'm okay," Janis said. "Really. I do feel terrible, though. This was supposed to be the happiest time of your life and . . . well . . . It's a mess, isn't it?"

"You're the best sister ever." As soon as the words left her, Susan widened her eyes and gasped. She blinked when tears filled her eyes. Putting her fingertips to her lips, she shook her head slightly. "Oh, I shouldn't have said that. Not right now."

Janis turned her hand over and squeezed Susan's. "It's okay. I know what you mean."

"I'm glad Mom didn't hear that," she whispered. "I'd never live that down."

"I have a feeling we'll all be walking on eggshells around her for the foreseeable future."

Misery settled over Susan's face like a shadow. Her shoulders slumped, and her mouth twitched like she was trying to hold in a sob. Her gaze dropped to their joined hands, and when she spoke again, her voice was barely above a whisper. "She's going to be unbearable."

The corners of her eyes glistened, and for a moment, her expression turned glassy and distant—like she was imagining every tense conversation to come, every guilt-laced comment, every reminder that Eunice was the one who mattered more. Because even Susan understood that Eunice had always been their mother's favorite.

Janis couldn't look at the pain on her face anymore.

Couldn't look at *her* anymore.

The view was breathtaking—shimmering under the late morning sun. Glistening waves rolled in slow, lazy arcs, their crests catching the light like scattered diamonds. A few fluffy clouds drifted across the azure sky, and palm trees swayed in the breeze as if dancing to a song only they could hear.

It was a picture of peace.

And for the first time in her life, Janis felt it.

While Susan wiped tears from her eyes and their mother no doubt plotted an entire life built around tragedy, Janis watched the waves and felt something close to calm.

There was no storm in her chest. No weight pressing her down.

Only silence. Freedom.

Eunice was gone—and the world, outrageously, was still beautiful. The calm should have made her feel worse. Should have sent her spiraling with guilt. But it didn't.

She didn't feel haunted. She felt *light*.

While everyone else mourned, she couldn't stop herself from wondering if this was what happiness felt like.

"It's nice here," Janis said.

"I'm glad you like it."

"Maybe you and Thomas can come back another time." When her suggestion was met with silence, Janis eyed her little sister. "Did I say something wrong?"

"No. Not at all," Susan said in a quiet tone. "It's just . . . Up until this morning, we had already started to plan to return next summer to celebrate our first anniversary. But I don't think I can ever come back here. This could never be a happy place for me. Even if I did get married here."

Something shifted in Janis's chest—not guilt, exactly, but a sharp awareness that she should feel *something*. Sympathy. Sadness. Regret.

She didn't.

Still, she softened her voice. "I'm sorry it was ruined

for you."

"It's not your fault," Susan stated firmly. She held tight to Janis's hand. "Listen, Jan, Thomas and I talked earlier, after you and Mom fell asleep, and we're both concerned she's going to try to take her anger out on you."

Janis didn't say anything. She didn't have to. *Of course* their mother would blame her. She always had. If something went wrong, Janis had been the built-in scapegoat for as long as she could remember.

It didn't matter if she'd done anything wrong—Phylis had a way of bending facts to fit the version of reality she preferred.

"I want you to know," Susan continued, "we're going to do what we can to protect you from that. From her. If you ever need me to step in and make her back off, please say so."

Janis looked down at their hands. Susan's fingers were warm. Steady.

"I won't let her blame you for what happened to Eunie," Susan whispered.

It was a sweet promise. But Janis wasn't sure Susan could stop what had already started.

"Now you're the best sister ever," Janis whispered and meant it. "But you don't have to protect me from Mom. I know how to handle her."

"But you shouldn't have to. Not after everything you've been through."

Thomas set two more plates on the table and then eased into the chair next to his wife. "We're here for you," he said to Janis in a soft, warm voice she'd never heard him direct toward her. It was enough to make her eyes burn from unshed tears.

"Thank you." Janis's gaze fell on the octopus on Thomas's plate, and she chuckled. "I tried that last night for dinner."

He looked up, surprised, then grinned. "Really? What did you think?"

"I think I'll stick with fruit and toast," she said, wrinkling her nose.

He laughed—a real, belly-deep laugh—and something fluttered in her chest. That familiar, aching tremble that always came when she made him laugh. It was the one thing that made her feel like she mattered in his orbit, like she existed in his world in some quiet, private way.

But the moment shattered almost instantly.

Susan squeezed her hand and laughed along, scooting closer to Thomas without even realizing it. "She has the worst luck with food," she said, reaching for her drink. "Remember Denver? She ordered squid ink pasta and nearly gagged at the table."

Thomas chuckled again. His eyes were warm with amusement.

Janis smiled, but it was thin. Fake. Susan hadn't meant anything by sharing the story—Janis knew that. But still, the sting was there. That casual way her sister could turn her into the punchline.

Janis hated how familiar that felt. Like Susan was already taking over the role Eunice had vacated. And how easily Thomas laughed along. The warmth from his attention cooled to ash in an instant. Reminding her that no matter how hard she tried, she would always be the one people laughed at.

Thomas turned toward Susan. Just like that, Janis was invisible again. That shouldn't have hurt. But it did. His warm voice, his easy smile, his effortless affection—none of it belonged to her. Not really. They belonged to Susan. And Susan didn't even have to try.

The pain struck Janis's heart quick and sharp.

She'd loved her little sister all her life. But in that moment, something in Janis shifted. Something she wasn't sure could be undone.

Because part of her—in that instant—started to resent Susan, too.

Chapter Five

Their room service had already arrived. There was no reason for anyone to knock on their door.

Unless it was the police.

Unless it was *finally* happening.

Sure enough, the same two officers who had questioned her two nights earlier stepped into the room. Their voices carried toward the balcony as they spoke to Thomas, but Janis couldn't make out what they were saying. Her heart dropped when Thomas turned to look at Phylis.

This was it. This was the moment. The one where they announced she'd been overheard whispering to a dying woman that she wasn't going to help. That she'd stood there and let her sister bleed out. This was when it all came crashing down.

She'd murdered Eunice, and somehow, Eunice would still get her way. Even after death.

"What's happening?" Janis asked, her voice dry and cracking.

"I'm not sure," Susan said, but the tension in her

shoulders indicated otherwise.

Janis's gaze flicked toward the water. For one brief, insane second, she considered scaling the railing, leaping into the surf, disappearing beneath the waves. That had to be better than prison.

Better than watching Thomas look at her like a stranger.

Their expressions were solemn, practiced, unreadable.

This was it. This was when they'd say it out loud. That she had let her sister die. That she hadn't even *tried*.

The woman officer gave a faint, respectful nod before speaking. "We wanted to let you know the medical examiner has confirmed the cause of death."

Murder. The word echoed through Janis's mind like a voice in a canyon, bouncing, reverberating, growing louder. Her brain snapped back to that night. Leaning over Eunie. Stroking her hair. Whispering a confession that no one else should've heard.

Her hands started to tremble.

This fear—this sick, curling dread—was worse than facing down a man with a knife. At least that kind of danger was *simple*.

The officer looked directly at her.

"The knife nicked the left ventricle of her heart," she said. "Every beat pumped more blood into her chest cavity."

Phylis gasped, long and dramatic, as if on cue.

Janis flinched but, for once, was grateful for the distraction.

"Mom," Susan murmured, rushing to her side. She placed both hands on Phylis's shoulders.

Their mother looked ready to hyperventilate, her

breath sharp and shallow. Then came the waterworks. She pressed her napkin to her face. "Oh, my poor Eunie!"

The officer waited a beat, then turned her attention back to Janis.

"I want you to know there was nothing you could have done for your sister," she said gently. "Staying by her side to comfort her was the right decision."

To comfort her. The words landed like stones. She hadn't comforted Eunie.

She'd watched her bleed. Watched her fade.

And still, somehow, she was being painted as the good sister.

Janis closed her eyes and lowered her face. The relief she felt had nothing to do with whether or not anyone thought she'd done the right thing. She was relieved that the officer hadn't outed her for not even trying to help her sister.

"I know this isn't easy to hear," the officer continued, "but Eunice's body will be released tomorrow. You can start making plans to return to the states."

"Do you need anything else from Janis?" Thomas asked.

Her name on his lips made her breath catch.

The question itself was simple, polite. But it cracked something open inside her. He was thinking about her. He was *protecting* her, in his quiet, dependable way. She hadn't even considered that the police might want something more from her—but Thomas had.

Thomas had looked at the officers and thought, *What about Janis?*

Her chest filled with flutters—tiny, foolish things that she tried to ignore, but couldn't. She hated how much it meant to her. That he'd said her name. That he'd thought to check.

"No. We have the video. If . . . *when* we find the man responsible, we will notify you. If Ms. Duke's testimony is needed, we'll let you know."

"You have my number," Thomas clarified. "I would appreciate it if you'd reach out to me. I can let Ms. Duke know. I think it would be easier for her to hear coming from family."

Family.

The word sank into her skin like sunlight. He wasn't answering for her—he was *protecting* her. Stepping between her and something hard and cold.

The woman looked at Janis. "Is that okay with you?"

Her throat was too tight for words.

It was more than okay. It was everything.

She felt as if she'd been wrapped in a warm cocoon. Thomas was standing there, in all his handsome glory, shielding her. Worrying about her. Putting her first.

She couldn't find the right words, so she simply nodded her head.

The officer returned her focus to Thomas. "I'll make a note that you should be our point of contact."

"Thank you," he said.

She turned to Janis one more time. "Contact us if you think of anything else that could help us find this man."

"We will," Thomas said.

We. He said *we.* Janis and Thomas. Once again, she lowered her face so she could get her feelings in check. No one had ever taken care of her like this. She was always the one taking care of everyone. She was the one who had to step back and let Eunie shine. She was the one who had to protect Susan from their mother's insanity. She was the one who had to placate their mother to calm her tantrums.

No one ever looked out for *her*.

But Thomas was. A blush warmed her cheeks as her breathing grew more difficult.

"It's okay, Jan," Susan whispered as she removed a hand from their mother's shoulder and put it on Janis's. "Everything is okay."

"How can you say that?" Phylis screeched. "Nothing is okay. *Nothing*."

"Mom," Susan started, "I meant—"

Phylis started crying so hard her shoulders began to shake—so violently that the movement transferred through her elbows, which were planted firmly on the table, her face buried in her hands. The table trembled with each sob.

Janis's tea splashed over the rim of her mug. She watched it pool into a golden puddle on the white saucer. It took everything in her not to snap at the woman.

For God's sake. No one else was making such a scene.

"I'm sorry for your loss," the officer said to Thomas before leaving.

Once they were alone, Thomas returned to the table and sat across from Janis. Without saying a word, he reached across the table and gently rested his hand over hers. Just for a second.

But it was enough.

His touch was warm. Grounding. *Real*.

Her breath caught, but she did her best to keep her expression steady—even as her heart thudded in her chest like it was trying to escape. That heartquake feeling took over her again. The one where she wasn't sure she wouldn't die from how fast her pulse was thumping.

"Thank you," she finally said. "I'm not sure I could handle having the police call me."

"You don't have to do this alone," he stated.

"It's not right." Phylis dropped her napkin and turned her narrowed tearstained eyes toward Janis. Hatred had drowned out the grief. "Nothing is going to be right ever again."

Janis didn't know what to say to that. Her world was infinitely better already. She'd gone nearly two days without a single criticism from Eunice. She'd gone nearly two days without her mother comparing her to her twin. And best of all—two days of Thomas looking at *her*. Speaking gently to her. Protecting her in front of the police. *Seeing* her.

Her world had never been quieter. Or freer.

She should've said something comforting. She should've offered a lie. But she couldn't.

For Janis, *everything* was right. Finally. She couldn't find the words to sympathize with her mother. She couldn't find the words to lie.

"If you had gotten help—"

Janis's breath hitched. The old rhythm returning. Her mother was reaching for someone to blame—and Janis was the only one left.

"*Mom*!" Susan cut in sharply, her voice tight with shock.

Janis had been expecting this. She didn't, however, think her mother would say such nastiness in front of witnesses. Usually, she saved that for when they were alone.

"We're not doing that, Phylis," Thomas stated calmly. He was always so serene. So steady. "The only person to blame here is the man who mugged them."

"You heard the police officer," Susan said. "She said nothing Jan could have done would have made a difference. She did the right thing by staying with Eunie. She was with her. That's all she could have done."

"You did the right thing, Janis," Thomas told her, his voice soft but unwavering as his gaze met hers.

Warmth flooded her chest. If he kept speaking to her like that—kept looking at her like she mattered—she wasn't sure how long she could go on pretending she didn't love him. Pretending she didn't need him.

She shifted closer. Barely an inch. Enough that her shoulder brushed his.

He didn't move away.

"It should have been you," Phylis seethed quietly.

"Oh my God," Susan shrieked. "Mother, that is a horrible thing to say."

"Phylis," Thomas stated, his voice sharp with disbelief. His face flushed red, and he shook his head, clearly trying to hold his anger in check.

Then, without hesitation, he draped his arm around Janis's shoulders and pulled her against his side. The contact sent a jolt through her chest. Her body stiffened for a moment from sheer surprise, but she quickly melted into the warmth of him—his solid frame, his reassuring presence, the faint scent of whatever soap he used that clung to the collar of his shirt.

She wanted to freeze time. To stay right here, with his arm wrapped around her, like it belonged there. Like *she* belonged there.

For so long, she had only imagined this closeness. Had built her longing in silence, brick by brick, while standing in his shadow. And now—here he was, anchoring her in a storm that had been her entire life.

Her mother's words still hung in the air like smoke, but Janis barely registered them now.

All she could focus on was this moment. For the first time in as long as she could remember, she didn't feel invisible. She felt *wanted*.

"That is *not* an acceptable thing to say. *Ever*," Thomas practically spat at Phylis.

Janis didn't speak. Didn't react. She could barely remember what her mother had said. With her heart pounding and her face burning, all Janis could feel was the weight of Thomas's arm around her shoulders. And all she wanted was for him to never take it away.

Then Susan let out a sudden sob. Thomas's arm stiffened.

And before Janis could even process the shift, he gently pulled away and rounded the table to Susan's side, where she'd covered her face with her hands. She was crying now—openly, quietly, the grief finally pushing through whatever composure she'd managed to hold.

Thomas wrapped her in his arms, murmuring something Janis couldn't hear.

Janis stood there, frozen in the empty space he'd left behind. The warmth that had filled her only seconds earlier drained away, leaving something hollow in its place.

Setting her napkin aside, Janis stood. "Excuse me," she whispered. She had barely stepped into the room before she heard Thomas admonishing her mother once again.

Finally. Someone was putting Phylis Duke in her place

The happiness she had been fighting spread across her face.

Eunice was dead. Her mother was unraveling. And Thomas—*Thomas*—was defending her. Speaking up for her. Choosing her in his quiet, dependable way.

Janis felt almost weightless. She might have killed her sister *sooner* if she'd known this would be the outcome.

Not that she *had* killed her. Not really.

It had been the knife. The blood. Eunice's failing heart. That was what had killed her. Janis had only stayed. Only watched. Only let it happen.

She wasn't a murderer. *Not exactly*.

She walked straight to the bathroom and closed the door behind her, letting her back press against it. The smile stretching across her face grew wider. Her body hummed with something that felt dangerously close to joy. She was on the verge of giggling when a knock sounded on the door.

She stiffened.

One breath. Two.

She wiped the smile from her face and cracked the door open. Her heart sank with disappointment when she saw Susan instead of Thomas.

Tears fell down Susan's cheeks. "She didn't mean that."

"Of course she did," Janis said. "It actually took her longer than I expected to say it."

"I'm sorry."

Janis shook her head as she opened the door wider. "Don't do that, Susan."

"Don't do what?"

"Apologize for our mother being . . ." She stopped before calling her mother a monster.

That word was too easy. Too tame. A monster was

scary. A monster was loud and dangerous. Phylis was worse than that. She was silent shame dressed up in pearls. She was cold disapproval served with a warm smile. She was the voice in Janis's head that always asked, *Why can't you be more like Eunice?*

"She's a soul-eater," Janis said, her voice low and flat.

Susan blinked. "A what?"

"A soul-eater. Norse mythology. They devour a person's essence, not their body. That's what Mom does. She doesn't kill you outright—she makes you believe you were never alive to begin with. I spent my entire childhood trying to win her love. And she—she just lashed out, undermined me, made me disappear until all she could see was Eunie. Until I was nothing."

Susan opened her mouth, then closed it. Even *she* couldn't defend that. Susan had received the same treatment, only not to the same extent. Being younger, prettier, and more charming had saved her from taking the brunt of Phylis's deranged sense of mothering, but she'd felt the sting all the same.

"I won't let her blame you," Susan finally whispered.

"You can't stop her."

"Well, I won't let her say things like that to you. Neither will Thomas. He's having a talk with her right now."

"He shouldn't. She'll turn on him, too."

"Let her. We don't care." Susan squeezed her hand. "We care about you. We're going to take care of *you*."

We.

Of course Susan and Thomas were a *we*. They were married. In love. Happy.

Janis had to force herself to acknowledge her sister's kindness. "I appreciate it."

"I'm going to ask Thomas to book us a flight home as soon as possible. I don't want to spend one more minute than we have to in this God forsaken place."

Janis nodded. "I'd like that."

Susan put her hand on Janis's cheek. "Don't let Mom's words get to you. She's grieving."

She was like this long before grief. The words rose in Janis's throat, sharp and hot, but she didn't say them. She was too tired to argue. Too tired to pretend Susan didn't live in some alternate version of their life—one where Phylis was flawed but forgivable. One where Janis wasn't always the afterthought.

"Thanks, Susan. And thank Thomas for me. He's been very kind."

"Well, he's a very kind man."

Janis bit back a reply. Something too warm, too soft, too caring. Something that would have given her real feelings away. She gestured toward the bathroom behind her. "I need a few minutes alone, then I'll be okay."

"Take your time," Susan said before stepping away.

Janis closed the door behind her, and let the silence settle like dust around her.

For a moment, she stood there, her back pressed to the door, her hand still on the knob like she might change her mind and go back out. But her legs felt heavy. Her chest tight in a way that wasn't grief exactly—but wasn't nothing, either.

She turned slowly toward the mirror. Her reflection looked back at her—drawn, pale, rimmed in exhaustion. Hair limp. Shoulders slightly hunched.

A woman who had watched her twin sister die.

She leaned in, searching for something in her own eyes.

Some flicker of the pain she was supposed to feel. Some trace of devastation.

But there was nothing like that.

There was only quiet. Not peace exactly. But not chaos either.

She wasn't numb. She wasn't heartbroken. She was something else entirely.

Chapter Six

Unfortunately—or not—Susan and Thomas had to cut their honeymoon short and go home with them. *Them* being Janis, their mom, and Eunie's body which was tucked inside a casket in the bottom of the plane.

As Janis sat, waiting to board, she stared at her hands. She couldn't stop staring at them. Three days had passed since they'd been covered in Eunie's blood, but she could still see the thick red coating her fingers and palms.

"Hey, Jan." Susan's voice had taken on that soft, coaxing tone—the kind people used with frightened animals or grieving children. She hadn't stopped using it since the police gave them permission to take Eunie's body home.

It should've been comforting. It used to be.

Once upon a time, when they were younger, when Phylis had been too sharp and Eunie too cruel, it had been the two of them. Jan and Susan. Clinging to each other in the shadows, whispering secrets and pinky-swearing survival. Susan's gentleness had been a lifeline.

Janis didn't understand why it was bothering her. She should've been grateful. But now, that same gentleness made her feel prickly. Raw. Like she was being handled.

Susan looked down at Jan's hands. Janis followed her gaze and—for a split second—saw them not as they were, but as they'd been. Crimson-soaked. Velvet-dark. Sticky with something she could still feel, even if it was long gone.

Susan reached out and wrapped her fingers gently around Janis's. Janis didn't pull away.

But she didn't smile back either.

"I'm worried about Mom," Susan whispered. "She says she's been having chest pains."

Janis barely batted an eye. She hadn't reminded Phylis to take her meds since the night Eunie died. Without her nagging, their mother tended to forget to take care of herself.

What a pity.

"I think I should sit with her," Susan continued. "I don't . . . I don't think you should be the one to take care of her right now."

Janis blinked. She hadn't even considered taking care of her. Not until that moment. Turning her gaze to where her mother sat, she watched Thomas whispering as he leaned close to her.

"I need you to sit next to Thomas on the plane," Susan said.

Janis blinked again. She couldn't stop the smile that touched her lips. But that wasn't the proper reaction, so she fought to keep the excitement out of her eyes and gave Susan a soft look to mirror the one she was receiving. That stupid it's-gonna-be-okay reassurance that always fell short in situations like this.

"Okay," Jan said.

Susan squeezed her hands. "Are you sure?"

"Yes."

"It's just that . . . Mom is . . ."

This time, when Janis turned toward their mother, she saw her wiping her eyes with the edge of a crumpled tissue. Silent tears. No dramatics. No shrill demands. Only soft, shuddering grief. Thomas was there beside her.

He pulled Phylis gently into his side, his arms folding around her in a quiet, instinctive embrace. Then he pressed a soft kiss to the top of her head—tender, intimate—and leaned close as he spoke. Janis had only seen him do that with Susan but now he was doing it to Phylis.

The kind of gesture Janis had never received. Something sharp and electric surged through her chest. Like a bolt of lightning with nowhere to land.

Thomas was comforting her mother. The same woman who had said Janis should've died instead. It felt like betrayal. But she understood. He wouldn't hold a grudge over something said at the height of grief. Not when he didn't know Phylis the way Janis did. Not when he didn't carry decades of invisible bruises from her.

Still, watching him show gentle, effortless kindness stirred something inside Janis she couldn't quite contain. She wanted that. She *needed* that.

Maybe if she cried—put on a show like Phylis—he'd look at her the same way. Maybe if she fell apart, he would hold her. She could do that. If that's what it would take.

Returning her focus to Susan, she nodded. "I think the doctor is right. I think I'm still in shock."

"And that's okay," Susan said. "Jan, it's okay. You've been through so much." Her voice cracked as tears filled her eyes. "I'll let Thomas know."

As Susan approached him, Thomas looked up and Janis met his gaze. His eyes were so tender, so filled with concern. She had this strange feeling inside—like her stomach was melting, softening into something unfamiliar. Like something she'd never dared to imagine might be within reach.

Before she had to decide what to do, a flight attendant approached and spoke to them in hushed tones, inviting them to board ahead of everyone else, even though they weren't first-class passengers.

On the plane, Thomas sat next to Janis and smiled supportively as they buckled their seatbelts. Her mom and Susan sat in the row in front of them. Though they were leaving the island behind, Thomas still smelled like sunshine and salt air. He smelled handsome. That might not have made sense, but that's what Janis kept thinking. Every time he'd move, she'd get a little waft of *handsome* washing over her. It caused her heart to do that quaking thing.

They sat in silence as the rest of the passengers filed past, the overhead bins snapped closed, and the attendants began their practiced instructions about oxygen masks and emergency exits. Janis barely heard a word. Her attention stayed on her hands in her lap—and the man sitting beside her.

Finally, the engines roared to life. The plane shuddered forward, and they were headed back to Kansas.

She still didn't feel like crying, but she reached into her purse anyway and pulled out a tissue. She dabbed gently at the corner of her eye. Then her nose. Enough to suggest quiet grief. Not too much—nothing dramatic.

Thomas wouldn't hear a sniffle over the engine noise,

but he would see the motion. And that was what mattered. As she'd hoped, every time she brought the tissue to her face, he reached over and gave her other hand a gentle, reassuring pat. Every. Time.

She would turn to him with a faint, grateful smile—measured just right—and he would smile back. That soft, sympathetic tilt of his lips that always made her feel like maybe she mattered.

And every time it happened, her heart quaked.

She felt seen. Tended to. Wanted.

She didn't know what unsettled her more: how easy it was to make him reach for her—or how good it felt when he did. Because she wasn't really crying.

Not yet.

But she was starting to learn how.

After the layover in Houston, Thomas and Janis were separated from Susan and her mom. Though the flight attendants tried to move seats around, they ended up several rows away. It was then, after they were in the air again, that he stopped the gentle patting and gripped her hand. She turned her palm to his and squeezed tight as their fingers entwined. Her chest filled with so much warmth she could barely breathe.

Was this what love felt like? This suffocating heat surrounding her? Was it love?

For so long, Janis had kept those feelings buried, stuffed deep beneath the weight of her twin's presence—her perfection, her dominance, her shadow. There had never been room to feel something this big. Something that didn't belong to Eunice first.

But now, for the first time in her life, Janis could feel something without worrying how Eunice would use it against her.

Without needing to hide. Or apologize.

Thomas was kind. Steady. The only person who looked at her like she was worth something without asking her to prove it.

She wasn't sure if it was love. But it was the first time in her life she felt like she might deserve it. And that made her want to hold on to it.

Even if it wasn't hers to keep.

He held her hand from Houston to Kansas City. His palm rested against hers, warm and steady, his thumb occasionally brushing lightly across her knuckles like it meant something. He didn't speak, but the silence felt full—comfortable. *Chosen*.

For a little while, Janis let herself believe it meant something. That she wasn't alone. That someone—*he*—might actually see her.

But the moment they stood to get off the plane and he reunited with Susan, the spell was broken.

Thomas let go of Janis's hand without a glance, like she had never mattered. He crossed to Susan, slid his arm around her waist, and leaned close to whisper something only she could hear. She tilted her head toward him.

Janis watched them—watched how naturally they fit together, how easily she was forgotten. A bitter ache filled her chest. Not jealousy, exactly. Not heartbreak. Just recognition.

This wasn't new. It had always been like this.

She'd spent so long blaming Eunie for being cruel, for stealing the spotlight with barbed words and loud ambition. But Susan—*Susan had taken as much*. Only Susan did it quietly. Sweetly. She didn't push Janis aside—she simply stepped in front of her and *stayed there*.

No one ever asked if Janis wanted to be seen. If she wanted to be chosen. They assumed she didn't. Because Susan was easier to love. Easier to hold. The warmth Janis had carried on the plane turned cold, like hard glass inside her chest. Thomas and Susan moved ahead without her. And once again, Janis was left trailing behind.

Not rejected. Forgotten.

"Now isn't the time," her mother said with a chastising tone.

Blinking, Janis pulled her mind from Thomas and Susan. "What?"

"They are married now. You'll have to accept that she has someone new in her life. Someone more important than *you*."

The scathing comment stung, but Janis didn't respond. She couldn't. Because if she opened her mouth, she'd say something she couldn't take back—something that had been building inside her for years.

She'd point out that it was *Phylis* who had sobbed the loudest. *Phylis* who had clutched her chest like she was on the verge of collapse, gasping and shaking for every ounce of attention she could wring from the room.

She'd say her mother hadn't simply grieved Eunie—she'd performed. Milked the situation. Worn her tears like a damn tiara.

But saying that out loud would start a war she wasn't ready to fight. Not yet. So she did what she'd always done—bit down on her tongue and kept her mouth shut. Let the poison pool at the back of her throat.

Only this time, the toxicity burned a little hotter. She wasn't sure how much longer she'd be able to swallow it down.

Her mother followed Susan and Thomas, leaving Janis seething in her frustration. Pushing her irritation away, she trailed behind her family.

As they stood at the baggage claim, watching the crowd tighten around the conveyor belt, Susan reached for Janis's hand. The gesture was almost identical to the way Thomas had held her hand on the plane.

But it didn't feel the same. It lacked the quiet electricity Janis had felt in Thomas's palm. It didn't stir warmth. It stirred obligation. Janis was so weary of feeling obligated. She wanted the freedom that she'd felt when she and Thomas had sat so close on the plane. She wanted that sense of belonging back.

Janis tore her gaze from where he was blending into the herd of people gathering their luggage. He looked capable, dependable, in command.

"Mom is going to stay with us for a few days," Susan said. "I think you should, too." Her words were gentle, reasonable.

But Janis heard the *invitation* beneath them. The idea of staying under the same roof as Thomas made her breath catch. Being near him, in the quiet of night, across the hall or across the kitchen table. Sitting in his home, sharing a meal, laughing over a story on social media. She could see them now. And it was perfect.

"For a few days," Susan added. "Maybe until after the funeral." Susan brushed a strand of Janis's hair from her forehead. The touch was light. What most would consider maternal. "I want you to know that you don't have to be the strong one this time, Jan. You've been through something traumatic. I'm here for you. I'm here to help you.

You *don't* have to be the strong one," she said again.

Susan had always been gentle in a way Eunie never was. If it had been *Susan* who'd died, Eunie would be screaming, pointing fingers. Blaming Janis. But not Susan. No, Susan was standing here offering support and comfort and grace.

Janis loved her sister. Of course she did. They'd been close for so long. When Eunie was cruel, Susan was her shelter. Her safe place. Her person.

But now Susan was standing between her and the one person who made her feel like she mattered. Her kindness no longer warmed Janis. It irritated her.

Shame pricked beneath Janis' skin.

"I think . . ." Janis started, but the words tangled in her throat. She forced a small breath. "Maybe it's better if you focus on Mom right now. I'll be fine."

Susan's soft smile dimmed. "Janis," she whispered, "I know you have a hard time being around new people, but Thomas is family now. He's kind. I promise. He'll help take care of us. All of us. Please, let us help you."

Us.

The word felt heavier than it should. Janis didn't know how to respond—to the offer, to the guilt curling in her gut, to the fact that her mind kept skipping back to the way Thomas's hand had fit over hers like it belonged there.

She didn't want to hurt Susan. She didn't even want to feel like Susan was standing in her way, that without her, Thomas would be where he belonged—with Janis.

But she did. She *did* feel that way. And that terrified her.

Still, she nodded. "Okay."

Susan's smile spread. "Thank you." She put her arms

around Janis and hugged her. "I love you."

"I love you, too," Janis whispered as she watched Su-san's husband lift a suitcase off the conveyor belt. That suitcase held Thomas and Susan's belongings. A second suitcase held Janis's, Mom's, and Eunice's things. Eunice had insisted they pack one suitcase so they didn't have so much to haul around.

That meant when they got home—to Susan's—Jan was going to have to sort through the bag so Eunie's hus-band could take her belongings. She glanced around, won-dering why Roger hadn't met them. She suspected he was home with the kids, consoling them.

Then again, Roger had never seemed overtly interested in his wife. Jan had considered many times that the reason her once popular sister had grown to be so bitter and judgmental was because she'd gotten herself trapped in an unhappy marriage.

Maybe if she'd been happier, she wouldn't have taken such pleasure in mocking Janis.

"Jan," Thomas said, breaking into her reverie.

She blinked a few times. "Sorry."

"It's okay," he assured her. Putting his hand to her back, he guided her toward the doors. Though she had no right to, Janis stood a bit taller with him by her side. For a moment longer, she could pretend that he belonged to her.

And that moment was perfect.

Chapter Seven

The condo Thomas and Susan shared only had two bedrooms. Janis wished she'd thought of that as she stared at the full-size bed she would be sharing with her mother. Though she thought she'd do almost anything to be close to Thomas, she wasn't in the mood to be nagged.

"You have to set aside whatever it is that's bothering you," her mom stated as soon as the bedroom door was closed, and they were alone. "We have bigger problems than your dislike of your brother-in-law."

"I never said I disliked him," Janis stated. "You and Eunie said I disliked him."

"Susan thinks you dislike him."

Sitting on the edge of the bed, Janis stared at a framed photo of an orchid in various shades of blue that matched the carpet and bedspread. Susan had bought the condo fully furnished before she and Thomas had started dating. She hadn't changed a thing. The entire space still felt like it had been staged by a real estate agent.

Susan loved it but Janis thought the condo felt cold

and uninviting. She liked the little house she shared with her mother. The house where they'd grown up. Though it was older and not as nice, it felt like a home instead of an advertisement for some overpriced building.

Janis ran her hand slowly over the down-filled duvet, her fingers smoothing the creases as if she could will softness into something that had none. This place—it was too polished, too curated. Nothing real ever happened in spaces like this.

Thomas deserved more than cold walls and bedding chosen by a stranger. He deserved warmth. He deserved *comfort*. He deserved a home that felt lived in, not one that looked good in a brochure.

Janis knew how to make a place feel like home. She knew how to listen. How to notice. How to give. Susan loved him, sure—but she didn't bring comfort and warmth. Not the way Janis did. Not the way she could.

Tuning out her mother's non-stop lecturing, Janis sorted through the suitcase until she found a clean nightgown and her toiletries. Her mom was still rambling as Janis stepped into the attached bathroom and closed the door behind her with more force than necessary.

The lights above the mirror were harsh—too white, too clinical. Janis blinked at the brightness and frowned. Susan really should have swapped the bulbs for something softer.

The unforgiving glare bleached the color from her skin, making her look ghostly.

Dead.

Like Eunice.

Janis leaned closer to the mirror. The hollows beneath her eyes looked deeper in the light, the skin stretched thin, tired. Her lips were bloodless, and the faint crease between her brows was more permanent than she remembered.

But it wasn't exhaustion. It was residue. The echo of a thousand tiny cuts left behind by words Eunice had wielded like weapons. Eunice often wondered how they could be twins when Janis was so incredibly flawed.

Janis could still hear the snide comments. Could still feel the way they'd settled into her bones, shaping the way she moved, how she smiled, how she *hid*.

The marks were still there. Faint. Invisible to anyone else. But Janis saw them.

Until suddenly, she smiled. Slow and sharp. The corners of her mouth lifted into something unfamiliar, something wicked.

Only then did she see a little life return to her face.

Never again would she have to tolerate Eunice's needling tone or her passive-aggressive digs. Never again would she be reminded—subtly, relentlessly—that she wasn't enough. Never again would she be second.

Her joy faded as the truth settled over her like a shadow. That wasn't quite right. Eunice might be gone, but *Phylis* was still here. And as long as her mother was breathing, there would always be someone waiting to step into the role of executioner. Someone to keep Janis small. To remind her that she'd never quite measure up.

A familiar heat rose in her chest—the same kind that used to spark in the face of Eunice's cruelty. Only now it had a new target. Her cheeks flushed. Her blue eyes hardened. For a second, she barely recognized the woman staring back at her. She looked dangerous.

Not like the timid wallflower. Not like the overlooked sister or the dutiful daughter. The woman in the mirror had a clenched jaw, steel in her spine, and a spark in her eyes that refused to dim.

"Not anymore," Janis whispered as her grin curved back into place. Calm. Controlled.

She brushed her teeth. Washed her face. Changed. And stepped back into the bedroom like someone returning to a battlefield.

"Take your meds," she said flatly, slipping easily back into the role she'd let slide since the night Eunice died.

Phylis didn't look up. "I need water."

Janis paused mid-step, the old reflex still in her limbs—still ready to fetch, to serve, to appease. But she stopped. Turned. Faced her mother and coolly said, "Go get some."

Her mother gasped, but instead of backing down, Janis flipped the duvet back to reveal crisp white sheets. Sterile. That was the word that came to mind.

"Excuse me, young lady."

Janis looked across the bed at her mother with one cocked brow. "I said, go get some."

Her mother lifted her chin a notch, staring down her nose at Janis. That look usually did Janis in. She usually caved because she couldn't handle the stress of confrontation. This time, however, she climbed into bed and pulled the covers up. She wasn't in the mood to get bossed around, especially when her mother was perfectly capable of getting a glass of water herself.

She didn't have to cross the Sahara. The kitchen was right down the hall.

Janis ignored the huff of indignation and the exaggerated stomping of her mother's feet as she walked away. Standing up for herself felt good. Really good.

A spark of satisfaction lit in her chest, sharp and sudden. She wished she'd done it sooner. Years ago. Maybe things would have been different if she'd pushed back.

But even as the thought crossed her mind, it fizzled. Because deep down, she knew it wouldn't have mattered.

The woman was as self-righteous as they came. She would never change, never see that her behavior was wrong. That was exactly where Eunie had learned it. She'd molded herself after their mother. Their superiority came from the same place: practiced, polished, and passed down like a genetic trait. Like their brown hair and blue eyes. Like the paleness of their skin.

Only this trait had skipped Janis and landed with Eunice in abundance.

Janis's sense of triumph fizzled away with the understanding that she hadn't really accomplished anything. All she did was set herself up for another lecture. Another tick on the checklist of why she wasn't good enough. She would be called ungrateful. Rude. Uncaring. Cold. Exactly like her father's side of the family.

She could already hear it.

Tossing the blanket off, Janis hopped up and rounded the bed. She eased her way to the door and listened. As she suspected, her mother was telling Susan all about how Janis had rebuffed her "request." She said *request* as if she'd actually asked. She hadn't. She'd made an order. One Janis had refused.

If she'd been asked, she might have complied.

"She's been through a lot," Susan said gently.

"I'm sure she's tired," Thomas offered. "She cried all the way home."

A strange flutter moved in Janis's chest at the sound

of his voice. Defending her. Again. But it was immediately drowned out by her mother's snappy reply.

"Stop making excuses for her. She doesn't deserve to be defended after the way she's acted."

"Mom," Susan said, "it's a glass of water."

"That's not what I mean."

Janis's heart nearly stopped. Without another thought, she rushed down the hall. "Mom?"

The conversation stopped and Susan offered Janis a smile. Thomas turned his back to her, busying himself with something on the stove, but Phylis rolled her eyes with theatrical flair and heaved a sigh so heavy it practically echoed.

"For God's sake, Janis, put something on."

The words hit like a slap.

"She's fine, Mom," Susan said like she was trying to soften the blow.

Janis looked down at her nightgown. The white cotton covered her down to her shins and the cap sleeves hid her shoulders. She was hardly revealing anything. Some of Susan's sundresses showed more skin. Yet, her mother's eyes were wide with faux horror, and her cheeks flushed as if Janis had come out nude.

Janis swallowed her fury, but it was rising fast—hot and bitter in her throat. "I don't have a robe here," she said. "I realized I was short. I didn't mean to be. Did you get your water?"

A look of superiority filled her mother's face. Smug. That was the word. She was smug, and Janis had never hated her more. Her hands balled at her sides, and she imagined how good it would feel to punch the condescending smirk right off her mother's lips.

"I did," Phylis snapped. "No thanks to you."

Janis's nails dug into her palms. She pressed her lips together, holding back the words that were clawing to be released.

Then, as she tended to do, her mother turned on the dramatics. Putting her hand to her chest, she sighed loudly and dropped onto one of the stools at the island as if she were about to faint. "If it were up to Janis, I would have dehydrated by morning." Her voice trembled. Her sigh was barely shy of a wail.

Janis felt something snap inside her. She no longer wondered if she hated her mother. She knew. Down the depths of her soul. She *hated* that woman. Hated her attitude, her face, her voice. Everything about her.

"Mom," Susan said gently. "It's not like you're bedridden."

Their mother's back stiffened and her mouth puckered at the insult. She didn't like being contradicted. Didn't like not getting the sympathy she clearly expected. But Janis didn't feel satisfaction. Not really. Because rage was still humming beneath her skin, steady and sharp.

She was tired of being embarrassed. Tired of being made small.

And right now, she felt like she might finally say something she *wouldn't* regret.

"We should get some sleep," Thomas interjected. "We have to meet Roger at the funeral home first thing in the morning."

Janis waited for her mother to walk down the hallway before shrugging. "Sorry," she said to Susan. "She was being bossy, and I wasn't in the mood."

"I know how she can be," Susan reassured her. "We

have to be a little patient with each other right now. We're all under a lot of stress."

When wasn't she patient? When wasn't she under stress? She lived her life trying to live up to Phylis's demands, calming her tirades, feeding her ego. Susan had escaped to this cold condo. She had no idea what the hell she was talking about.

Forcing herself to give a nod, Janis simply said, "Good night."

Susan pulled her into a tight hug.

Warm. Familiar. Janis let herself sink into it for just a second—long enough to pretend they were still sisters, still close, still on the same side of the glass.

"I love you," Susan whispered, and then she pulled away and disappeared down the hall with Thomas.

Janis swallowed hard. He hadn't turned back. He hadn't wished her a good night. He hadn't looked at her. She looked down at herself—the plain cotton nightgown, stiff from detergent, shapeless and soft in all the wrong ways. What kind of sleepwear did Thomas like?

Silk? Lace? Something barely-there?

Susan would know. Of course she would. Janis would have to find a way to check her drawers—for reference. Not to copy. Not *really*. Just to know. In case Thomas ever saw her again like this. In case there was a moment.

Following her mother, Janis eased the door shut behind her and turned off the overhead light. The lamps on the nightstand offered more than enough light for her to get to bed. She started to ask her mother if she'd taken her meds, but there was no glass of water on the nightstand.

Of course there wasn't. She must've left it in the kitchen. Or forgotten entirely.

Janis stared at the empty space on the table. Then climbed into bed without a word.

She's not my problem. The thought came loud and clear. Cold. Satisfying. She wasn't her mother's keeper. Not anymore. She didn't have to be. If Phylis forgot her meds again? So be it.

Let her heart race. Let her chest ache. It wasn't Janis's responsibility to fix it.

She fluffed the pillow, settled onto her side, and closed her eyes. No "good night." No small talk. No tending to her mother's needs.

Only the dark. And the silence. And the strange sense that something inside her was changing. Becoming stronger. Becoming who she had always been deep down.

Chapter Eight

The funeral home was like a vacuum. As soon as she stepped inside, Janis felt the life being sucked out of her. The space was unnaturally quiet and dim, like a void waiting to be filled with grief.

Roger, Eunie's usually cold husband, heaved a big sigh as if he sensed it as well.

Susan slipped an arm around their mother's shoulders, directing her forward. Thomas, without a word, placed his hand at the small of Janis's back—the same way he had at the airport. Her breath caught in her throat. Warmth bloomed under his touch. She looked up at him. She didn't say anything, afraid that even a whisper might break the moment.

The door had barely closed behind them before a man in a charcoal suit and dark blue tie padded toward them. He held his hand out to Roger, who shook it limply but failed to introduce anyone else. He always had been rude.

Thomas stood beside her as the funeral director guided them toward a room lined with gleaming, open caskets. His thumb made a slow, absent pass across her back. Just once. The man in the suit spoke in hushed tones as he asked Roger questions about Eunie and if he had any preferences on color or style.

While Susan and their mom whispered their suggestions to Eunie's widower, Janis pretended to study the caskets but could barely focus. Satin, wood grain, bronze handles—none of it mattered. It was going to be under six feet of dirt anyway. What was the point in agonizing over the finish and the color of the lining?

"Doing okay?" Thomas asked in a quiet voice meant only for Janis to hear.

She jolted slightly, surprised by his question. She slanted her gaze and offered a nod for an answer. He must not have slept well the night before. There were dark circles under his eyes. She didn't want to think about what might have kept him up too late. Though Susan was mourning her sister, they were still newlyweds. Janis might not know what it was like to have a passionate interlude with a man, but she had no doubt that Susan did. And with Thomas.

The thought made Janis's spine stiffen.

"Should we step out?" Thomas asked. "I don't think they need us here."

A genuine smile tugged at Janis's lips. "Please," she whispered.

Thomas finally pulled his hand from her back and took a step forward to whisper in Susan's ear. Immediately, her mother turned toward Janis and narrowed her eyes in that judgmental way Janis had come to loathe. Only now, she didn't care what her mother thought of her. She didn't flinch or shrink or correct course. Phylis and her judgmental thoughts could go to hell. With Eunice.

Thomas closed the distance between them and put his hand on Janis's arm. His touch made her skin buzz. She turned and let him guide her from the room. Her pulse was loud in her ears. Her steps too quiet. But for the first time in days, she felt . . . alive.

He chose to leave with her. That had to mean something.

The room where the funerals took place was lined with rows of stiff chairs, but there was no casket on the platform at the front of the room. Not yet. Eventually Eunice would be on display there. The center of attention. Everyone would line up to praise her. To whisper stories about how kind she was, how beautiful, how *irreplaceable*. They'd hand out hollow accolades like they handed out Halloween candy, completely unaware of who she'd really been. She would be the star of the show even in death.

Janis would sit in one of those chairs, listening to a litany of lies. Pretending that Eunice's death wasn't the best thing that had ever happened to her.

But for now, the room was quiet and they were alone.

"Sit," Thomas said. He squatted down and looked up at her. "Can I get you some water? I saw a drink station in the lobby. How about some tea?"

The tenderness in his voice undid something in her. She was touched. Deeply. Moved by the care he continued to show for her.

Warmth spread through her. A cowlick of dark brown hair tempted her to soothe it down, the way he was soothing her. She started to lift her hand, to gently stroke his hair back into place, but stopped herself at the last moment. As much as she wanted to care for him, that was a step too far. Even she knew that. Instead of touching his hair, she patted his hand. "I'm okay, Thomas. Thank you."

He gripped her hands in his. "I want you to know that I'm here for you, Jan. We're family. You can ask me if you need something."

She studied his face—the soft lines of it, the concern in his eyes, the way he spoke with such quiet conviction. We're family. The words should've stung. Should've snapped her back into place. But they didn't. Instead, they made her want to cry.

Or maybe kiss him.

"I appreciate that."

He gestured toward the room where the rest of their family were shopping for Eunie's casket. "I know this has to be a lot after what you've been through. You're being incredibly strong, but you don't have to be."

Her throat tightened. He was saying all the things she had spent three years wanting him to say. She turned her hands so that she could hold his hands as he'd been holding hers. The intimacy of it wasn't lost on her. The warmth of his skin settled into her bones, quieting the ache that had been lodged there since the night Eunice died. "Thomas, I—"

She didn't even know what she was about to say. That she didn't feel strong? That he was the only one who had made her feel real? That he was the first person who had made her feel seen in her entire life?

The sound of a throat clearing stopped her before she could say anything. They looked to where the funeral director had come into the room supporting Janis's mother. Thomas stood immediately, brushing his palms on his jeans, oblivious to how the moment had nearly unraveled into something more.

Janis stayed seated, pulse thrumming in her ears.

The spell was broken. But the memory of his hands in hers lingered like a secret she wasn't quite ready to let go. Disappointment filled Jan's chest as she listened to her mother panting for breath. The brief moment between her and Thomas had been so perfect, so intimate. Of course, her mother had to ruin it.

The sound of her short breath irritated Janis to the point of grinding her teeth.

Janis would have loved to tell her mother to stop her dramatics and go back to planning Eunie's funeral, but Thomas wouldn't possibly understand the raw resentment she held for her mother. Instead, she patted her mom's knee.

The older woman sniffed and held a tissue to her eyes before looking up at her son-in-law. "I'm fine. A bit short of breath."

Thomas squeezed her hand. "You're doing the best you can."

"Yes." She turned her attention to Janis. "We've selected a casket. Jan, you need to go give Susan your thoughts. She wants to make sure you're in agreement."

Janis's resentment grew. Not only had her mother interrupted her moment alone with Thomas, but she was forcing Janis to leave them alone. As she had the night before, she feared her mother would tell Thomas the lies that she and Eunie had fabricated. However, she couldn't come up with a single good reason to stay seated.

"I'll walk with you," the funeral director said kindly.

Janis wanted to argue, but logic won out. She slowly rose and walked beside the director to the room where the caskets were lined. Susan choked back a sob as she gestured for Janis to come closer.

As Janis stood over the walnut-stained wood box with the shiny white satin lining, she pictured Eunice lying there for eternity. Perfect hair, polished nails, smug expression wiped clean. The image nearly caused her to chuckle, but she held it in.

Her fingers grazed the smooth satin. Soft. Cold. Elegant in a way Eunice had always pretended to be. Now she would be here. Frozen.

Janis ran her hand slowly over the material, and the image shifted in her mind. It was no longer Eunie lying in the box. It was their mother.

Finally still. Finally incapable of sneering or scoffing or tearing Janis down with a single arched brow. Janis's breath caught in her throat.

No more questions about her weight. No more comparisons. No more accusations whispered under the guise of concern.

A memory snapped into place—so fast and sharp it stole the breath from her lungs.

She was seven. Maybe eight. She couldn't remember what she'd done—forgotten to iron her dress or tracked mud into the hallway—but the punishment was swift. Her mother had dragged her by the arm, shoved her into the linen closet, and slammed the door.

"You need to learn how to think about what you've done," Phylis had said from the other side.

No light. No sound. Just shelves pressing in on her. The scent of old fabric and lemon polish. Her small fists pounding until they ached.

She'd sobbed until her voice was hoarse, certain she'd suffocate in the dark. She'd stayed in there until the sound of Eunice's laughter finally cracked through the silence.

They'd left her there. For hours.

Now, standing in front of this box, Janis realized something. She hadn't been afraid of the dark that day. She'd been afraid of being forgotten.

Eunice was the one who would be forgotten now. Slowly. Over time. People would stop mourning. Stop remembering. And she'd fade away. As if she'd never existed in the first place.

"What do you think?" Susan asked with an emotion-thickened voice.

Janis blinked. The image in her mind—the closet, the silence, the coffin—blurred and folded in on itself.

She looked down at the casket again. "It's perfect," she whispered. "It's absolutely perfect."

Janis tried—truly tried—to be interested in the details being shared about Eunie's funeral. The flower arrangements, the readings, the music. None of it felt real to her. A window dressing for a performance she'd refused to participate in.

She had declined the opportunity to speak at the funeral, insisting it would be too much. Everyone seemed to understand except her mother, but that was usually the case. Phylis had looked at her like she'd failed some unspoken test. Again.

What amazed Janis most was how little she cared.

She felt oddly untethered. Maybe it was numbness. Or maybe it was freedom.

Thomas had supported her decision to stay seated during the service. He'd even said she'd done a good job of setting a boundary and reinforcing it when her mom tried to guilt her into telling Eunie's friends and their family how wonderful she'd been.

"You'll regret it, Janis," her mother had said. "You'll wish you'd said something when you had the chance. What kind of sister stays silent?"

But Eunice hadn't been wonderful. Not to Janis. And Janis wasn't going to stand before a room full of familiar faces and rewrite history for their comfort.

After dinner, she headed to Susan's guest room, hoping to have a bit of time alone. Her nerves were frayed, her mind buzzing, and the last thread of self-control she had left was beginning to unravel.

For some reason, as soon as they'd returned to the condo, Thomas had stopped whispering supportive words and gently touching Jan and had turned his attention to Susan. Every time he put his hand on Susan's or said something under his breath to her, Janis felt a burning in her chest that was building into a furious fire. She needed to get away before she said or did something to embarrass herself.

However, she wasn't so lucky. Her mother was on her heels. Janis snatched her nightgown from the foot of the bed and escaped into the attached bathroom, dragging out her nightly routine to buy a few extra minutes. But when she returned, her mother was there—perched on the edge of the bed, arms stiff, mouth already puckered with disapproval.

"What's wrong with you?" the older woman snapped as soon as Janis stepped into the room.

"What?"

"Your sister is dead, and you can't be bothered to say a few kind words for her?"

Janis didn't answer right away. She moved calmly, almost serenely, pulling back the covers. "Why don't *you* stand up and say a few kind words?"

Her mom huffed. "Because it will be too difficult for me."

She stopped moving and eyed the woman who she had come to hate as much as she'd hated Eunie. "Yet that isn't a good enough excuse for me."

"She was your *twin*."

"She was your *daughter*."

They stared at each other, decades of disappointment, silence, and judgment thick between them. Janis could almost hear it, humming like a live wire.

Her mother blinked first. "I don't understand you. I never have."

"You've never tried." Janis climbed between the sheets and rested her head on the pillow. She turned her back to her mother, face toward the wall, eyes open to watch the moonbeams cast dull shadows. She wasn't sure what stung more—Thomas slipping away, or the truth of what her mother had said.

But the sting was turning into something else now. Something sharper.

"What does that mean?" her mother barked, her voice pinched and shrill.

"Let it go, Mother."

"You will not speak to me like this."

Janis sat up slowly, turned, and met her mother's glare with a calmness that was terrifying, even to her. "You speak to *me* like this all the time. You and Eunice have treated me like a joke all my life. Every word, every look, every back-handed compliment—it was all to remind me I'd never be good enough. That I was always *less*."

Her mother opened her mouth, but Janis didn't give her the chance.

"Well, guess what?" she said in a cold, even tone. "Eunie's gone, and I refuse to spend the rest of my life letting you treat me like I'm less than some dead body that will be rotting away. Eunie's always been your favorite, your little shadow. Well, your shadow is dead, Mom, and I am finally free from her torment." She could no longer contain how happy that made her and a sinister smile spread across her face. "I'm free." She let the words hang in the air. They tasted like honey. Like truth. The smile didn't last long. Her face hardened like cooling metal. "And I won't be tolerating your bullying anymore. So deal with it."

With every word she said, her mother's jaw had sagged, and her eyes had widened until she looked like she belonged on the poster for a horror film. Her shock was comical, and Janis laughed softly. Pathetic old woman.

Janis laughed. A real laugh. A light one. The kind people use when they finally understood the joke—and realized it was on someone else.

"I . . . I don't understand."

"Because you're an idiot."

That did it.

The color drained from her mother's face as she clutched her chest. Her breath hitched—gasping, uneven. She stared wide-eyed at her daughter, but Janis didn't move. Not even after her mother cried out and fell to the floor.

"I'm not catering to this show of dramatics," Janis said. Her heart pounded, but it wasn't from panic. It was adrenaline. Power.

Clarity.

She should have done this years ago. What was it that Thomas had called it? Setting boundaries. Oh, this was good. This was so good.

"Stop. Right now."

When her mother didn't respond, Janis rolled her head back to look at the ceiling.

"Mother. I'm not playing this game with you. Not tonight. Not ever again."

Still nothing.

The silence dragged. Uncomfortable. Endless.

Finally, Janis stood and stepped toward the limp figure on the floor. When she got close enough, she could see her mother's face had drained of all color. Her eyes fluttered. Mouth parted. Her breath coming in short wheezes.

The pallor wasn't an act. The sharp, wet rattle of her breath wasn't something that could be faked. A grin pulled at Janis's mouth, slow and twitching. Anger had never tasted so sweet.

"Help me," her mom pleaded through clenched teeth, the sound barely louder than a breath.

Janis didn't move. She simply stared down at her—the woman who had spent a lifetime shrinking her, silencing her, molding her into someone easy to ignore. Hatred surged in Janis's chest like a furnace cracking open.

"That's what Eunie said too," she stated coolly. "'*Help me, Jan.*' As if she hadn't spent her entire life making mine miserable. As if I owed her something for the years of cruelty I had to endure. '*Help me, Jan,*'" she said again in a mocking tone. She crouched, knees creaking as she lowered herself to eye level with the suffering woman on the floor. "She didn't deserve my help," Janis said. "And neither do you."

A flicker of something flashed in her mother's eyes—recognition, maybe. Or terror. Or understanding. The same horror that had bloomed across Eunie's face that night now washed over Phylis, and Janis laughed. She didn't try to stop it. Couldn't, even if she wanted to.

She stood tall again, looming, and then reached down. Her mother whimpered as Janis grasped her wrists—thin, papery skin slick with sweat—and began walking backward, slowly, dragging her around the bed. Phylis's heels thudded against the carpet. Her breath came in shallow gasps.

Janis didn't flinch.

When they reached the far side of the bed, Janis dropped her mother's arms, and then peeled the blanket back. "It's time for bed, Mother."

She leaned down, wrapped her arms around the dead-weight of her mother's torso, and heaved. Her muscles strained. The effort made her jaw clench and her back burn. Phylis's body was soft, heavy, uncooperative. But Janis didn't stop until she got her into bed.

Her mother groaned faintly as Janis tucked the blanket up beneath her chin with clinical precision. Then Janis sat on the edge of the mattress, taking in the sight of her. Sweat glistened across her forehead, tiny beads catching the lamplight like dew on porcelain. Her lips were pale. Her chest rose in shallow, uneven hitches.

Janis reached for a tissue and dabbed at the moisture. Gently. Tenderly. "You're all tucked in now," she whispered. She leaned forward and pressed a kiss to her mother's clammy cheek. Her lips lingered a second too long. "Good night," she said, almost sweetly, before reaching over to turn off the bedside lamp.

The clouds overtook the moon and darkness enveloped the room, dim and intimate. She rounded the bed without a word. The only sound was the unsteady wheeze of her mother's breath as Janis slipped beneath the covers on the other side, her movements unhurried, deliberate.

Her body stilled, but her mind did not. She lay there, eyes open, listening to the fragile rasp of the woman beside her.

Chapter Nine

The next morning, Janis slipped from bed without a glance at the still form beside her. The room was cold. Quiet. Too quiet. She didn't check for breath.

She didn't need to.

She showered slowly, methodically, letting the water wash away the sweat and whatever guilt might have clung to her skin overnight. There wasn't much guilt to wash away. Not really. What remained was something sharper. Lighter. Liberating.

She dressed in the same clothes she'd worn the day Susan helped her change out of the borrowed scrubs in Mexico. Somehow, it felt right. Like a costume that had been waiting for its final act. She hadn't been back to her house since the trip. And though she suspected Susan and Thomas would let her linger a bit longer in the guest room out of sympathy—or obligation—Janis also knew the countdown had begun. But there'd be an extension. There always was, when death struck.

Susan didn't know it yet, but she'd soon be grieving

their mother, too.

And grief? That bought time.

"Good morning," Janis said as she walked into the bedroom. She smirked when her mother didn't answer. "Still sleeping? I'll leave you to it then."

She eased the bedroom door closed behind her and walked to the kitchen where Thomas was pouring coffee. He looked so natural there. So *belonging*. The image of him standing at her kitchen counter flitted through her mind, uninvited but welcome.

"Where's Mom?" Susan asked as Janis sat at the table.

"Still sleeping," Janis said. "I'll wake her after breakfast."

"I'll get her." Susan started to stand.

Janis grasped Susan's hand. "Let her sleep. She tossed and turned all night." Her voice was calm. Her hands were steady. But inside her mind, something had shifted entirely.

And it wasn't coming back. She liked the new version of herself. The Eunie-free version. Soon to be Mom-free, too. There would be no one left to undercut her. No one left to tell her she wasn't good enough or to treat her like a petulant child. She could just be now. Herself. Janis Duke.

She didn't know who that was, but she was eager to find out.

Would she be stronger? Happier? More confident.

Somehow she suspected she would be all of the above.

Thomas set a mug with a tea bag in front of Janis. Her fingers curled delicately around the warm ceramic, savoring the heat. "Earl Grey for the lady."

She smiled, probably more than she should have. "Thank you."

"Your toast will be ready in a minute. Fig jam, correct?"

"Yes, please." Janis forced a woeful look onto her face, glanced at her sister. "I suppose we should decide when Mom and I will go home."

Susan glanced at Thomas, then looked back at her. "Actually, we were talking about that last night."

We. Always *we*. Janis didn't flinch, but a small fissure cracked inside her chest.

"I think we should stop by the house and get you and Mom some fresh clothes. I've taken the next two weeks off work for bereavement. I'd like you and Mom to stay until after the funeral. Is that okay?"

Janis stirred her tea, watching it swirl. A soft clink. Again. And again. The tinkling was quiet. Subtle. But annoying. Like Susan's overly attentive cooing had become. Had she forgotten that Janis was the older sister? That Janis was the caretaker? That Janis had a mind of her own.

Always butting in where she didn't need to be. Always overstepping. She thought she was better because she hadn't taken the brunt of Phylis's abuse. But did she ever stop to think that was because it was *Janis* who had protected *her*? Why the hell was she treating Janis like a child?

But then she looked to Thomas who had stopped focusing on the toast to give Janis an encouraging smile. When she hesitated, he said, "It seems like we should be together right now. To help each other through this."

"I think that might be a good idea. I'm still not feeling quite like myself yet." She intentionally gave her sister a bashful smile. "I've been a little short with Mom. I don't mean to, it's . . ."

"I know how she can be," Susan whispered and then wrinkled her nose at Janis. As if she were speaking to a toddler. "I'll do more to run interference over the next two weeks so you can find some time to rest."

Thomas added two lightly toasted pieces of bread and the jar of fig jam on the table in front of Janis before taking the seat next to her. She felt the heat of him—close, attentive—and her heart stuttered with something that felt suspiciously like triumph.

But then he glanced at Susan. A look passed between them—quiet, heavy. *Aligned*.

Susan cleared her throat and offered yet another sad, condescending smile to her sister. "Thomas and I were talking—well, I was thinking really . . ."

Jan stiffened as she felt it. The shift. The trap. Kindness always came with a price. She was about to be told what that was.

"Janis, after everything you've been through . . ." Susan continued. "Would you consider counseling? I have a wonderful therapist, and I think she could really help you."

Janis sat taller as a chill ran through her. The tea turned to ash in her mouth. "Help me with what?"

"Processing your grief and trauma. You saw Eunie—" Susan's voice cracked, and she put her fingers to her lips.

"What you witnessed was incredibly frightening," Thomas said. "Susan thought it might help for you to talk to someone."

Janis turned her gaze on him, sharp as a knife. His words echoed through her with an almost physical sting. Thomas was siding with Susan. He was saying Janis was weak. That she was the broken little thing Eunice always mocked. How could he say that? How could he betray her like that? He was the one who always saw her. He was the one who understood her.

Anger twisted in her gut at Susan's suggestion. She didn't need therapy. She didn't need some stranger picking her brain apart. Thomas sat back under her scrutiny. He almost looked ashamed. As if he hadn't meant what he'd said.

"It was my idea," Susan said.

Of course it was. Of *course* it was Susan. Thomas would never betray her like that. Never. Not him. He understood. He was kind. He cared. He'd made her tea.

But Susan? Susan was the betrayer in disguise. A softer version of Eunie. She didn't try to break Janis down with fists and insults, but with careful words and concerned smiles. The kind that cut deeper than any blade.

Of course she wanted Janis in therapy. Of course she wanted someone else to poke around in her head and figure out what she couldn't control.

Janis smiled sweetly, and her voice came out light as air. "I appreciate the suggestion. I'll think about it."

But she wouldn't. She didn't need a therapist.

She needed Susan to back off.

And soon, she would.

"I'm going to check on Mom," Susan said. "It isn't like her to sleep this late."

Janis nodded but said nothing. She focused instead on spreading the fig jam carefully across her toast, covering every inch like she was smoothing over something broken.

Once she and Thomas were alone, she let her voice dip into that soft, uncertain tone she knew he responded to. "I know she means well," she said, "but I don't think talking to a stranger would help."

"She's so worried about you, Jan," he said kindly. He leaned a little closer, ready to share something that was between them, and whispered, "Don't tell her I said anything, but you've always been her favorite sister."

Janis met his eyes, her own widening with a gentle sort of wonder. She leaned in, mirroring his intimacy. "She's always been mine, too," she said, her voice featherlight.

Then she pulled back, her smile faltering enough to sell the sadness. "My relationship with Eunice was"—her smile faded and she sighed—"complicated."

Thomas nodded, and for a moment they sat there, alone in their shared stillness.

Janis took a small bite of toast, chewed delicately.

"Well, if you would consider talking to someone, even once, it would help ease Susan's mind. And mine."

Janis nodded again, slowly, as if she were truly considering it. "Well, I'm glad to hear that Susan has a therapist to help her through this. I mean, after how she fell apart when our father died, I can only imagine what this will do to her."

Thomas creased his brow. "What do you mean?"

She opened her mouth to reply. Innocently. Shocked. *Oh, didn't she tell you? Oh, I shouldn't say anything . . .*

Then Susan's scream shattered the quiet.

"Thomas! *Thomas!*"

He bolted from his seat and sprinted down the hallway without hesitation.

Janis didn't move at first. She calmly reached for her napkin, dabbed the corners of her mouth, and brushed the crumbs from her fingers.

She waited a beat. Then another.

Only when the sound of frantic voices filled the hall-way did she rise, smoothing her hands over her lap. Then she walked slowly toward the panic, prepared to be devastated by their mother's untimely death.

Chapter Ten

Anxiety clawed at Janis's chest as she sat rigid in the hospital waiting room beside Susan. The sterile air smelled like disinfectant and despair, and the flickering overhead light buzzed loudly enough to gnaw at her nerves. Thomas had gone to park the car, but every second he was gone felt like a thread unraveling.

She still couldn't believe her mother had survived.

Stupid, she thought. *So stupid to think she'd die in her sleep.*

She should've done it herself—held a pillow over her mother's face, pressed down hard. She should have finished what had been started. But she'd hesitated. Because she'd hoped the universe would do her dirty work.

Now, she had a problem.

If her mother woke up, she would tell everyone. About Janis standing over her. About the refusal. The mockery. Janis would deny it, of course. Feign horror. Paint her mother's story as the confused ramblings of a woman unwell. But would Susan believe her?

Would *Thomas*?

That was the real fear.

Susan rested her head on Janis's shoulder. "What are we going to do if Mom dies, too?"

The weight of her sister's touch felt too intimate—too heavy. Janis kept her gaze trained on a scuffed spot on the linoleum. "We'll be okay. We'll take care of each other."

"And Thomas," Susan said with a gentle voice. "It seems like you're warming up to him finally."

Clenching her teeth together, Janis ignored the sting of Susan's words. Words that were far too reminiscent of the accusations her mother and Eunie had made. "I've always liked Thomas. Eunie and Mom were the ones always insisting that I didn't."

Sitting back, Susan eyed Janis who finally managed to turn her gaze to her sister. Susan had a look of disbelief on her face. Janis turned, meeting her sister's gaze head-on.

But Susan didn't speak. Didn't smile. Her brows pulled together as if trying to piece something together. As if she'd noticed a puzzle with too many wrong pieces.

The look on her sister's face indicated Janis had let something slip. She forced a frown, an uncomfortable shift in her posture. "Just because I struggle with speaking to people doesn't mean I don't like them," Janis stated firmly.

"I know," Susan was quick to say. "I'm sorry. I guess I misinterpreted your distance, too. I assumed you didn't care for him. I won't say anything like that again."

"Thank you."

"I didn't mean to make you feel bad."

Janis shook her head as if to dismiss the notion. "This week has been—"

"Horrific," Susan finished.

"Like I said at breakfast, I'm not quite myself right now."

"Me either." Susan put her head back on Janis's shoulder. "I really hope Mom pulls through. I don't think I can do this again so soon."

No, she thought, *you probably couldn't.*

Everyone had always assumed Janis was the fragile one—the anxious one, the one who crumbled under pressure. But they were wrong.

Susan had always been the one to fall apart. Janis remembered it all too well—how broken her sister had been after their father died. Susan had barely gotten out of bed. She cried so hard for so long that her face had stayed puffy for weeks. And who had to sit by her? Who had fetched her tissues, brought her food, told the school Susan was too sick to come in?

Janis.

She had barely processed her own grief because she'd been pulled into Susan's orbit, expected to help hold her sister together. To be the quiet, steady one. The afterthought with the stitched-on smile. And she'd done it. Because she'd loved Susan.

But now it all felt different.

Janis stared at the scuffed floor and felt her jaw tighten.

While Susan leaned in for comfort, Janis realized she no longer wanted to be the one her sister leaned on. She didn't want to hold her up anymore. Not when Susan already had someone else to do that now.

And not when all Janis wanted was for that someone to be hers.

"Me too," Janis lied.

When the elevator doors opened, Thomas stepped out

and scanned the waiting room until he spotted Susan and Janis. He eased into the chair next to his wife. In her peripheral vision, Janis watched him take Susan's hand and squeeze it tight.

That hand. That hideous little claw of a hand with her fake nails and tanning bed orange tint. Susan's fingers were short, papery things. Wrinkled at the knuckles. She'd once burned herself cooking. The scar was gnarled and ugly across the back of her hand. And now here Thomas was, curling his beautiful fingers around hers.

Janis's hands would feel so much better. Softer. Smoother. Warmer. He would feel the difference immediately. He had to know that. Didn't he?

"Any word from the doctor yet?" he asked.

"Nothing," Susan said. She shifted in her seat so she could see him more clearly. "I'm so sorry," she muttered.

"For what?" he asked.

"This certainly isn't the right way to start a marriage."

Sympathy flickered across his features, and then he draped his arm over her shoulders like it was second nature. His fingers slid through her limp brown hair, and he tugged her in gently to press a kiss to her head.

That effortless blend of strength and gentleness—like a man carved from marble but warmed by sunlight. His thick brown hair always seemed artfully tousled, not messy, but soft enough to touch. His eyes were a deep, warm brown—steady, kind, impossibly sincere. And that skin, naturally kissed by the sun, golden in a way Susan tried to replicate with tanning beds and bronzer but never quite got right.

Everything about him was real. Honest. Steady.

And an enigma. Because why was he with *Susan*? Of

all people?

Janis's eyes lingered on his profile—his straight nose, strong jawline, the gentle slope of his cheek when he smiled. There was no part of him that hadn't been etched in kindness. No part of him that hadn't, at one time or another, looked at *her* with warmth.

That's what made it worse. She *knew* what it felt like to be on the receiving end of that softness. She'd tasted it. Hints of it. Enough to make her want more.

So watching him now, his arm around her sister, comforting her like it was the most natural thing in the world?

It was unbearable.

She didn't want to watch him comfort Susan. She didn't want to see his mouth anywhere near her sister. It wasn't fair. Susan didn't even *appreciate* him. She didn't know what it was like to *need* Thomas. To feel seen by him. To feel *chosen*.

And wasn't that what burned the most? That Susan was the one he chose. Always, always Susan.

Janis could feel something bubbling beneath the surface of her skin—hot, acidic, dark. Like bile made of jealousy.

Her gaze flicked toward the nurses' station in time to catch the doctor glancing in their direction. He said something to the nurse who nodded and picked up the phone. Then he looked back at them again—but didn't come over. He turned and walked away instead.

Janis stood without thinking, every nerve in her body on alert.

What was that about?

Was he avoiding them? Hiding something?

She glanced back at Thomas, who was still whispering

something into Susan's hair, like a goddamn lullaby. Her stomach twisted.

He should be saying those words to *her*. Janis was the one who needed him now.

She had to look away and tune them out. As she did, she noticed the doctor who had been treating their mother at the nurse's station. He glanced toward the family as the nurse picked up the phone. Janis swallowed hard, watching, trying to determine what he was saying. She stood, barely breathing, as he looked back at them again. He didn't come to them, however, he turned and walked away.

Susan took Janis's hand. "Did you see that?"

Janis nodded. "What do you think that's about?"

"I don't think it's good news, Jan." Susan looked like she might fall apart right there—trembling, pale, so consumed by grief she could barely stay upright.

Janis watched her sister's fragile expression with a curious detachment, then carefully wrapped Susan's hand in both of hers, steady and strong. "It'll be okay, Susan," she whispered. "I promise. Thomas and I will take care of you."

The words slipped out so easily. So smooth. So *perfectly placed*. She turned toward Thomas, letting her eyes brim with concern, her voice quivering the right amount. "Won't we?"

Thomas looked at her and nodded. "Of course we will."

The warmth in his eyes. The quiet assurance in his voice. Her heart fluttered at the unspoken promise. She had *him*. In that moment, he wasn't her sister's husband—he was *hers*. Her partner in this new responsibility.

Her safe place.

Her heart quaked at the solidarity, the sweet vow they'd made. She and Thomas would take care of Susan.

And wasn't that fitting?

Susan was falling apart. Like she always had—after their father died, after every little bump in the road. Janis had been the one to pick up the pieces, to hold her together. Susan might have been the sweet one, the one people always adored, but when things got hard? She collapsed. She broke.

But not Janis. Janis endured. Janis survived. Janis could *take care* of people.

Thomas would see the difference. The strength Janis had. How deeply she cared. How weak Susan was.

She would make sure of it.

Chapter Eleven

Janis stood at the foot of her mother's hospital bed. Machines beeped around them, steady and constant, like the ticking of a countdown clock. Phylis had been in and out of consciousness, according to the nurse who had left the room. She hadn't been awake long enough to rat Janis out.

That should have been a relief. But it wasn't. It left Janis in a dangerous limbo. A waiting game she couldn't afford to lose.

The doctor had been optimistic. "A full recovery is expected," he'd said, as if that were good news.

Susan had let out a loud exhalation of relief, gripped Janis's hand, and put her other hand over her chest like she'd been holding her breath for days. "I'm so happy to hear that," she'd said.

Janis had faked a smile and echoed the sentiment, nodding like it was the best news she'd heard all week. But she'd lied.

She was *terrified*.

Because when Phylis woke up—really woke up—she would talk. She would tell them everything. She'd say Janis had mocked her, ignored her pleas, stood over her like a predator instead of a daughter. She'd describe it in vivid detail, twist every truth into something venomous. Janis could see it already—the narrowed eyes, the knowing looks, the soft, slow horror spreading across Susan's face. Thomas's, too.

She'd be finished. Everything she'd carefully constructed—her place in their grief, her closeness with Thomas, her role as the quiet survivor—would all unravel the moment Phylis opened her mouth.

And the worst part? They would believe her.

Phylis had always been good at that. At turning her disapproval into gospel. At spinning her disappointment into absolute truth.

Janis's stomach twisted. Her gaze flicked to the IV line, the wires, the machines. If only she could guarantee that Phylis would stay quiet. Permanently.

Her hand twitched at her side, fingers curling the tiniest bit.

She wasn't a murderer.

Not really.

But she was running out of options.

Once Jan and Susan were alone, Susan sank into the chair next to the bed and took their mother's hand. Though Phylis wasn't alert at the moment, Susan had patted her hand and said, "Do you hear that, Mom? You're going to be fine. You need some time to recover, that's all." Susan looked over her shoulder at Janis and her happiness faded. "Janis," she said softly, "she's going to be okay."

Janis nodded and forced her face to relax. "Yes. I heard

that as well."

"Then why do you look so stressed?" She gave a short laugh. "I mean, I suppose Mom being in the hospital is cause enough, but . . . Is something else bothering you?"

"I, um . . ." Janis hesitated, then sighed, carefully layering her voice with weariness. "I don't want to burden you, Susan. Not when you've recently married."

"Nonsense," her sister said firmly. She crossed to Janis and placed a reassuring hand on her shoulder. "What is it?"

"Did you mean what you said? That you'll help me more with Mom?" Janis looked down at the floor, making her voice small. "Because . . . Well, I can't force her to take her medications or to eat right or to exercise more. I've tried, Susan. I swear, I have. She simply won't listen. If she's going to need long-term home care, I don't know that I can do that alone. Not again."

Susan put her hands on Janis's shoulders and held her gaze. "You are not alone. And if Mom refuses to take her meds or eat less red meat, well, that's her decision to make. You aren't her mother or her nanny. You are there to help her, not force her to do anything. If she wants to fight you, then throw your hands up and let her win. And I did mean what I said. I'll be there to help you. If we have to, we'll hire a nurse."

Janis let the tension in her shoulders melt into gratitude—or at least the illusion of it. She smiled wider, even let her voice quaver a little. "Thank you. That eases my mind more than you know." She turned slowly toward the hospital bed as Phylis stirred. Her fingers moved against the sheet. Her lips parted slightly, brows twitched.

Janis's smile froze.

Her heart began to pound—not with affection, not

with longing, not like the *good* heartquakes Thomas stirred in her.

No, this was different. This was the *bad* kind. The heartquake of exposure.

Because when Phylis opened her eyes, she wouldn't be groggy for long. She'd speak. And the words wouldn't be kind. They never were.

Janis's clenched her fists at her sides. She braced herself—ready for the storm to come.

Susan turned as well. "Mom?" she asked as she returned to her seat. "Mom, it's Susan."

Phylis blinked a few times before mumbling incoherently.

Moving to the other side of the bed, Janis took the woman's other hand, squeezing tighter than necessary. "I'm here, too," Janis said as sweetly as she could. "I'm right here, Mom."

Her mom jerked her head to one side, then the other, mumbling as she did. Her heart monitor started to beep faster as she squirmed.

"Mom?" Susan asked. "What's wrong?"

"Maybe we should get a nurse?" Janis suggested.□

Susan pressed the call button on the side of the bed. "Mom, relax. You're okay. You're in the hospital. You had a heart attack, but you are okay. Tell her, Jan," Susan pleaded.

Janis leaned closer to the woman in the bed. She smiled when terrified eyes met hers. "Susan's right. You had a heart attack. I'm sure everything is confusing right now, but you're going to be fine. Everything will be fine."

A nurse rushed in and shooed Susan from the side of the bed. Speaking to the patient, she did her best to reassure her, but Phylis was panicking. "We're going to have to sedate her," she said to Susan. "Try to keep her calm. I'll be right back."

"Breathe, Mom," Janis advised. "Take a long, slow breath." She inhaled through her nose, and blew out through her mouth, trying to get her mother to mimic her.

Phylis turned away, focused on Susan, and mumbled again. This time it was more precise. Something . . . something . . . *help*. While nothing else had come out clear, the word *help* was.

"The nurse is getting help," Susan assured their mother in a sweet voice. "Calm down, Mom. Please relax."

Phylis shook her head and tried again, but her words were still nonsense—garbled syllables caught in her throat. Her eyes widened with frustration, then with fear. Desperation.

And Janis wasn't far behind her.

Her mother's lips kept trying to shape something meaningful. Janis could guess what it was.

Help me. Janis didn't help me.

A cold sweat broke across her back.

Phylis let out a raspy sigh, and Janis saw the exact moment she realized she couldn't make herself understood. That she was trapped inside her own body. Her fingers grasped helplessly against the thin hospital blanket, and her wild, watery eyes locked on Janis.

A silent accusation.

Janis's heart slammed against her ribs, panic crawling up her throat like bile. Her mind spun, frantic. *Why didn't I make sure she was dead?* Letting Susan find her was a mistake. A stupid, stupid mistake. Now here she was—alive, angry, and fighting to form words that would destroy everything.

Janis shifted on her feet, her hands clammy.

The nurse returned. "Step back, please."

Janis and Susan obeyed, silently moving away from the bed. The nurse inserted something into the IV line with calm efficiency, and within seconds, Phylis sagged against the pillows. Her jaw slackened. The muttering stopped. Her hands stilled.

Peace, finally.

Janis exhaled so sharply her shoulders dropped with it. "That was terrifying," she said, managing to infuse her voice with enough shaken concern to make it sound real. Because it was real, only not for the reasons anyone would think.

Susan nodded, eyes fixed on their sedated mother.

"We'll keep her under for now," the nurse said. "She needs rest."

"Thank you," Susan whispered, reaching for Phylis's hand.

Janis watched, silent. Cold. *That woman would burn the world down if it would make me look bad.*

And now Janis had only a matter of hours—or days—to figure out what to do about it.

Once they were alone, Susan turned wide eyes toward Janis. "I'd like to go home now. Are you ready?"

Janis nodded and shuffled behind her little sister toward the door. Once Susan stepped out to the hallway, Janis looked back. The faux concern on her face fell away as she narrowed her eyes, wondering how in the hell she was going to get rid of her mother before that bitch ruined everything.

Jealousy surged through Janis like a rising tide as Thomas held up a spoon, his eyes crinkling with warmth as Susan opened her mouth, eyes closed in anticipation. "What do you think?" he asked as his wife licked her lips.

Susan moaned softly, tilting her head like a blissful child. "Amazing."

Janis turned away, the heat in her chest burning hotter than the sauce on the stove. Her elbow brushed the wicker basket on the counter. On purpose. The basket tipped and spilled its contents—pens, stamps, receipts—across the kitchen floor with a clatter.

She gasped, masking the act with a surprised smile. "Sorry. I was trying to slip out unnoticed."

Susan crouched down to gather the scattered items. "You don't have to sneak around, Jan."

Kneeling as well, Janis gathered a roll of stamps. "I didn't want to intrude," she said, glancing over at Thomas. "I know you two need alone time. I was coming to ask if I could borrow a sweater."

Concern filled Susan's eyes as she looked at her sister. "Is it too cold? I can bump up the temperature."

"No," Janis insisted as she put the items she'd gathered back into the basket. "I'm always chilled. You know that. My cardigan needs washing and I . . ." She stood and set the basket aside. "I should probably go home and do some laundry."

"Nonsense," Susan stated. "I was already planning to do laundry tomorrow." She stepped forward and, in a sisterly gesture that had once made Janis feel safe, tucked a strand of hair behind Janis's ear. "Go grab a sweater. Take whichever one you want. They're hanging in my closet."

The touch was meant to comfort, but it made Janis flinch inside. The gesture felt invasive. Possessive. As if Susan were reminding her of her place in her house. In *her* family.

"Thanks," Janis murmured.

"Jan," Thomas called from the stove, "I'm making my grandmother's pasta sauce. Want to try it?"

Her heart did that little quaking thing at the thought of him feeding her as he'd done with Susan. "Sure," she said and smiled bashfully.

As she neared Thomas, the rich, savory aroma of the sauce made her stomach flutter. Or maybe that was being so close to him. His profile was sharp, backlit by the kitchen light. Brown hair that curled slightly at the ends, a jaw that could have been sculpted from marble, warm brown eyes that belonged to a man from a fairy tale—strong but soft. Safe.

He reached into the drawer beside the stove and pulled out a spoon.

Janis held her breath.

But instead of dipping it into the sauce and feeding her like he had with Susan, he extended the utensil in her direction. The gesture was polite. Distant.

The kind of thing you'd do for a guest, not someone special.

Disappointment rose in her chest like frost spreading across glass. She masked it quickly, forcing a gracious smile as she accepted the spoon. He stepped aside to give her space and put his arm around Susan's shoulder as they both watched her like she was an animal on display at the zoo.

Of course he wasn't going to feed her. Not with Susan right there.

Janis dipped the spoon into the simmering pot, blew on it, and slid the sauce into her mouth. The tang of tomato and garlic, the sweetness of the reduction, the warmth of basil and red pepper was exquisite.

Thomas was handsome. He was thoughtful. He remembered how she liked her tea. He opened doors without thinking. And now he proved himself to be a culinary artist. He really was everything.

"Well," he said, "what do you think?"

"It's wonderful, Thomas." Her voice was steady, but inside, something knotted. Something shifted.

Being on the outside watching her sister living the life she wanted was no longer acceptable. That would never be enough. Not now. Not after being so close to him, having him protect her, console her.

She needed more.

He smiled, beaming with pride. He removed his arm from Susan and closed the gap between him and Janis as light filled his eyes. "My grandmother didn't leave a recipe. She always said she cooked from the heart so there was no need to write anything down. I've been trying to perfect it for years."

"I think you got it," Susan offered, reinserting herself into the conversation.

Janis swallowed down the resentment she felt at that moment. Thomas had been talking to *her*. He had been sharing his excitement with *her*. Not Susan.

Janis put her spoon in the sink and nodded. "I agree.

It's delicious."

She watched as Susan slid to her husband's side, and he wrapped his arm around her. A bitter taste filled her mouth, turning the lingering aftertaste of his sauce into something sour. "I'm going to go grab a sweater," she whispered.

"I'll call you when dinner is ready," Susan said.

Janis nodded, her face neutral, and turned to leave. But once she was outside the kitchen door, she paused. Footsteps silent, she eased back against the wall.

"She seems to be doing better," Thomas said quietly.

"I think having some space between her and Mom is exactly what she needed," Susan answered. "I don't want to push her to go home with everything that has happened, but she was right—I am ready to spend some quality alone time with my husband."

Janis closed her eyes.

Then came the soft, unmistakable sound of lips meeting. Wet, lingering. Intimate.

A breathy moan followed. Feminine. Familiar.

Janis's eyes flew open. Her stomach twisted like wrung-out cloth. Rage boiled low and thick inside her gut.

"Your husband is looking forward to that, too," Thomas muttered, his voice dipped in a husky, private tone that made Janis seethe.

Grinding her teeth, she forced down the scream rising in her throat. Knowing what "alone time" really meant—that they would touch, that Susan would gasp into his neck while he whispered things only a husband should—made Janis's stomach turn over. Not with jealousy, but with nausea. Rage.

She fisted her hands, digging her short nails into the

skin of her palm, welcoming the sting. Anything to keep herself grounded. Anything to keep from screaming as she stalked down the hallway. Her steps were silent, but her mind was loud.

She paused outside the bedroom, glancing back down the hallway.

It'd be just like Susan to scurry along behind her to help her find the perfect cardigan. Like Janis couldn't figure that out for herself. Susan had always been a nuisance like that—trying to be helpful but getting underfoot.

Why couldn't she leave? Go spend the evening with friends or at the hospital. Why couldn't she give Janis and Thomas "alone" time?

After yanking the closet door open with more force than necessary, Janis shoved the hangers aside, seeking the section of the closet where Susan kept her sweaters. She found a thin gray button up and pulled it free. She didn't slam the closet closed because she didn't want Susan to come investigate, but she did shove her arms into the sweater like a petulant child.

She was about to storm out of the bedroom when her gaze fell on the chest of drawers. Her stomach tensed as she recalled how she'd wondered what kind of nightgown Susan wore. What kind of sleep attire Thomas preferred to see her in. The curiosity burned. An ache she couldn't ignore.

She tiptoed to the bedroom door and leaned out. Laughter echoed faintly down the hall—warm, easy, domestic. A knife in her heart. Janis eased the door shut and turned back to the dresser.

The top drawer slid open with a whisper. Inside: lace, silk, satin. Everything Janis had never dared to buy. Underthings that weren't meant for comfort—they were for performance. For pleasure. For men.

Susan's bras were delicate, structured but feminine. The lace overlay was soft against Janis's fingertips. She held one up by the strap, examined the stitching, then traced the cups with a kind of reverence. These weren't practical. These were for Thomas. These were for showing off.

She pulled out the matching panties and frowned at the sliver of fabric that passed for coverage. A thong. Of course. She wondered if Eunice wore things like that, too. Maybe. She'd always had that same effortless confidence Susan had. That same natural way of belonging in her body. Janis didn't. She never had. But maybe that could change.

Maybe it had to.

Janis closed the drawer and opened the next. She exhaled at the rows of folded nightgowns—satin, lace-trimmed, some barely opaque. She picked through them like she was choosing a costume, a disguise. She settled on a dusty rose gown with thin straps and a plunging neckline. It was modest enough not to look desperate, but soft enough to look feminine.

She folded it neatly and tucked it under her arm. But before she turned to leave, her eyes drifted back to the top drawer. Her hand hovered for a moment, then she opened it again and plucked out the bra and thong she'd studied earlier.

They didn't look like *her*, but maybe they could. Maybe she didn't need to be herself anymore.

Maybe being Janis had never worked.

Maybe being someone Thomas wanted was the better path forward.

Crossing the hall to the guest room, she closed the door behind her and went into the bathroom, locking the door behind her. She didn't think Thomas or Susan would walk in on her, but she wouldn't take the risk. In a rushed silence, Janis undressed with trembling fingers.

She held up the barely-there underwear, pinching the delicate fabric between her fingers as if seeing them clearly might change how foreign they felt. Another woman's lingerie. Her sister's lingerie. But Janis was tired of being the woman no one noticed. She wanted to know what it felt like to be wanted. Desired. *Chosen*.

Sliding the panties up her legs, she adjusted the narrow waistband and scowled as she maneuvered the back strap into place. It was uncomfortable, the kind of discomfort that came from trying on someone else's life. She shifted side to side, testing how it moved with her. Every step reminded her that it wasn't hers. Not yet.

But she moved on, adding the matching bra.

Black lace, scalloped edges, soft and daring all at once. She'd never owned anything so delicate. So bold. She fastened the hook, adjusted the straps, and stepped back from the mirror.

Her breath caught.

She would never consider herself sexy—Eunice had always been the beautiful one, Susan the sweet one—but in this moment, something had shifted. The mirror offered a version of Janis she didn't recognize. Covered in lace, back straight, collarbone peeking through her thin skin, she didn't look invisible. She looked kind of ... pretty.

Not beautiful, no. But *appealing*. Like someone who could be looked at. Wanted. Like someone a man might reach for.

Lifting her hair, she twisted it into a bun and secured it with a clip she'd taken from Susan's vanity. She leaned in closer, tilted her chin, and freed a few wisps of hair to frame her face. Then she tried. Tried to look sultry. Tried to see herself as someone Thomas might look at and not turn away.

But her mouth felt awkward. Her lips trembled. Her eyes didn't smolder—they pleaded.

She dipped her chin, narrowed her gaze. Sexy. Confident.

Ridiculous.

The word hit hard. She could hear Eunice in her head, laughing like she had in middle school when Janis had worn lip gloss and asked if she looked pretty. *"You? Please."*

Her confidence dissolved in seconds. The moment evaporated, and shame slithered back in.

With a frustrated grunt, she yanked the clip from her hair and let it fall around her face. She rubbed her palms over her cheeks, flushed and hot. Her chest tightened, and her throat burned with the sting of failure.

But then she paused.

She looked again.

There was something there—beneath the shame, behind the old voices.

A flicker of power.

This version of herself, half-dressed in black lace, was uncomfortable, yes. But she wasn't weak. She wasn't meek. And Thomas had never seen her like this.

Yet.

Janis stood up straighter. Maybe she wasn't trying to be someone else. Maybe she was becoming someone new.

With her hair a mess, standing in nothing but lacey

garments, she looked . . . like a woman. She looked like a woman a man might want to be with. Her stomach fluttered as she considered that this might be what Thomas was after. This might be what he wanted.

Sexy clothes and mussed hair. If she were wearing makeup, she might look better. She might have to ask Susan to teach her about blush and lipstick.

For a moment, she thought she might be able to pull it off. To present herself to him like this. To offer herself to him. She slipped the nightgown on over the undergarments. The satin clung to her, highlighting her waist while the thin bra pushed her breasts against the plunging neckline that was also lined in black lace.

Janis lightly trailed her fingers over the border, tickling her skin.

Suddenly, the illusion cracked, and she realized she didn't look pretty. She looked, as Eunice would have said, *pathetic*.

Thomas would never want Janis the way she wanted him. He'd never look at her and forget the rest of the world. He'd never kiss her. He'd never hold her in that soft, absentminded way that people do when they're in love. He'd never feed her with a spoon and wait with anticipation for her reaction. He'd never slide his arm around her waist, draw her close, and make her feel like she belonged to someone.

No one ever had.

She'd dated a few times. But they were awkward encounters built more on obligation than desire. A coworker who asked her out because he thought she "seemed sweet." A friend of a friend who took her to dinner, only to spend the night checking his phone. A library patron who flirted once and ghosted her after one coffee.

She'd never had a real relationship. Never been kissed like it meant something. Never had someone memorize her laugh. Or whisper to her in the dark. Or hold her hand in public because they wanted the world to know she was theirs.

She'd always blamed her shyness. Her awkwardness. Her lack of confidence.

But deep down, she knew better.

She wasn't the kind of woman men chose. She was the one they overlooked. The one who stood behind her dazzling sister. The one who stayed quiet. Who waited for a moment that never came.

And now, staring at her reflection—bare shoulders, lace edging her skin, her eyes a little too wide, her lips pressed too tightly—she saw the same woman. The one nobody had ever stayed for.

Still, something inside her refused to look away. She might not be beautiful. She might not be lovable. But she was *done* being invisible.

Her rage was real. All-consuming.

The kind that scratched at her ribcage and begged to be unleashed. But with Eunice gone, Janis didn't know where to put it.

And yet, the rage remained. Stronger. Louder. She needed someone to blame. She *wanted* someone to blame.

With no one else to blame, her gaze landed on Susan. Too kind. Too perfect. Too easy to love. Susan, who could weep and be comforted. Who could say nothing at all and still have Thomas's hand reach for hers.

No matter what she did, no matter how soft her voice or how sweet her smile, as long as Susan existed, Janis would never be the one Thomas looked to for affection.

She closed her eyes as she heard Eunie's voice bounce through her mind. "You will always be second."

"Janis," Susan called from the other side of the door. "Dinner's ready."

Closing her eyes, Jan let out a slow breath before calling out. "I'll be right there."

Returning her attention to the mirror, Janis scanned her reflection again. The woman staring back at her didn't look like the mousy librarian people overlooked. She didn't look invisible.

She looked like someone who *could* be wanted.

She reached for the nightgown, yanking it off with frustration that flared hotter than she expected. It landed in a crumpled pile at her feet. She stood there in Susan's lace bra and barely-there panties, chest rising and falling, pulse fluttering like wings under her skin.

She started to remove the undergarments, too, but then stopped.

No.

She wouldn't take them off. She'd wear them to dinner. Thomas wouldn't know. *But she would.*

She would sit across from him, smiling, pretending to be the grateful sister—humble, sweet, recovering from trauma. And beneath the surface, beneath the cardigan and quiet demeanor, she would be wearing *this*.

And she would know it was for *him*.

That thought curled inside her like a secret flame—dangerous and intoxicating. Her skin tingled, and something dark and powerful stirred inside her.

Sliding her short-sleeved dress over the lace, she added the cardigan then put her house shoes back on and ventured out to the kitchen.

She smiled as she sat at the table. "Thomas, this looks wonderful," she said as he put a plate in front of her.

"I hope it tastes wonderful, too." He filled a wine glass for himself before showing the label to Janis. "I picked up this Cabernet Sauvignon in Italy last year. Genuine Italian wine. Would you like a glass?"

Though Janis wasn't much for drinking alcohol, she nodded. "Thank you."

"I didn't know you liked wine," Susan said.

Janis shrugged as she eyed her sister's glass of water. Rather than pointing out that Susan wasn't having wine, she let this be one more moment—one more thing she shared with Thomas. "It's been a long few days."

"You can say that again," Thomas said sitting next to his wife. "I hate how much you both have been through." The stress on his face was obvious. He genuinely did care.

Janis's heart practically melted in her chest. Could this man be any more perfect?

He'd cooked for them. Thoughtfully selected wine. And even if his words were meant for both of them, they *landed* in her. Nestled in deep.

She took the glass of wine, sipped carefully, and let the warmth of it coat her throat.

Susan chatted beside him—something about how grateful she was for him, how lucky they were to have each other—but Janis barely heard it. All she could do was stare at Thomas as he talked to his wife and placed a hand on hers. That small, unconscious touch.

"I wish I could make this easier for you," he said his voice round and soothing, like it was stroking her cheek.

It felt like he was speaking only to her. Her lips parted.

She was about to thank him, maybe even let something real slip through, but Susan beat her to it. She slid her hand over his and leaned in to press a soft kiss to his cheek. Intimate. Effortless.

Rather than say anything, Janis drew a long, slow breath through her nose, the kind meant to tether a person to their last thread of composure. Her jaw tightened as she dropped her gaze to her plate. She reached for her fork with a little too much force, causing the metal to scrape loudly against the porcelain.

She twirled her fork far more than necessary to get the noodles around the tines—twisting and twisting as if the movement might tangle her frustration into something manageable. Then, after shoving the bite into her mouth, she focused on chewing.

Chew. Swallow. Smile.

It was the same routine she'd perfected as a child—swallowing down the things she wanted. The things she couldn't have. The things she wasn't allowed to feel.

While she forced her expression to remain neutral, her mind was anything but. The echo of Susan's kiss burned behind her eyes. Her stomach churned—not from the wine, not from the food—but from the fire slowly spreading through her chest.

She stabbed another bite of pasta, slower this time.

One day, she promised herself. One day, it would be *her* hand on his. Her kiss on his cheek. Her name on his lips.

And Susan would be the one left watching.

"Susan said the hospital visit was stressful," Thomas said.

Janis lifted her gaze to him and swallowed. "Mom seemed to be confused. It was hard to see."

"That's not uncommon for someone who has been through so much trauma. She'll come around." He gave his wife a sweet smile. "I'm sure of it."

When he turned his smile to Janis, she smiled in return. "I hope so," she whispered.

She took a sip of the wine, letting the liquid sit on her tongue a second too long. The bitterness hit her palate like an insult. She winced as she forced the liquid down.

"Oh," Susan said with a laugh, "you don't like it?"

A streak of hot anger flared under Janis' skin, sharp and blinding. She hated being laughed at. Hated it. It had always been their favorite game—Eunice and their mother. From the time she was small, they'd found sport in her discomfort, her awkwardness. The time she wore the wrong shoes to a school concert. The way she mispronounced "ḥors d'oeuvres" at a dinner party. How she held her fork wrong or couldn't name the label of the wine someone brought over.

"Oh, Janis," Eunie would say through giggles. *"You're like a toddler at a gala."*

Their mother would follow it with a faux-sympathetic sigh and a thin-lipped smile. *"She's trying her best, bless her heart."*

It was never simply laughter. It was humiliation, served in polite tones and condescending smiles.

Now Susan. Laughing like she didn't know exactly what that kind of condescending laugh did to Janis.

Janis's tightened her fingers around the stem of her wineglass. She forced a soft laugh of her own, light and airy. "Guess I've never developed the taste for it," she murmured, then took another sip—this time without flinching, even as the bitterness made her stomach turn.

She would not give her the satisfaction. Not again. She turned to Thomas and smiled sweetly. But then he laughed, too.

The heat behind her eyes was instant. Shame and fury rose to her chest like smoke. But she did what she'd always done—what she'd been *trained* to do. She smiled. Sweetly. Politely. Tightly. Like she used to when Mom and Eunice would make her the butt of their jokes and call it "teasing."

"I'm not used to it," Janis said softly. She took another sip and did her best to mask her dislike of the wine. "That's all."

"You don't have to drink it," Susan said.

"I don't mind."

Susan reached for it with that same effortless authority Eunice used to wield—like she was helping, like she always knew best. "I'll get you some ice water."

"No," Janis said, grasping for the glass as Susan's fingers brushed the stem. Her motion was too fast and she knocked the glass sideways.

The dark red wine spilled, bleeding across the pale tablecloth like a wound.

"Damn it," Janis snapped, her voice sharper than she intended—or maybe exactly as sharp as she wanted it to be.

Susan flinched, her hand withdrawing. Her eyes, wide and startled, locked on Janis.

"I said it was fine," Janis seethed, her voice quivering now—not with regret, but with the pressure of all the unsaid things tightening in her throat.

"It's okay," Thomas said quickly, rising from his seat.

He reached for a towel near the sink. "It's only a spill."

But Janis wasn't looking at the wine.

She was staring at Susan. At the soft, startled expression on her sister's face. At the way she shrank back, like Janis had lashed out at her for no reason.

Janis gave her head a firm shake as she realized her mask had slipped. That was the ultimate crime. Showing emotions was wrong. Very wrong. "I'm sorry, Susan. I—" Her gaze dropped to the crimson puddle creeping across the fabric. "That's how Eunie's blood spread."

The silence in the room fractured.

Susan gasped audibly as her hand flew to her mouth. Her already wide eyes somehow grew larger, glassy with fresh horror. Thomas stood behind her, frozen with the towel still clutched in his hand, his jaw slack.

Janis blinked, painfully aware of what she'd said. "Oh no," she whispered. "I'm sorry . . . I didn't mean to say that. I don't know what came over me." She shook her head again, more frantic this time. "I'm sorry."

Thomas stuttered. "It-it's the trauma talking, Jan. It's okay."

Big tears welled up and spilled down Susan's cheeks, and she started to speak but no words came. Finally, she whispered, "You still need time to process what you saw." But she didn't sound convinced. She sounded horrified.

Janis folded her napkin with shaking fingers and set it neatly beside her plate. Her appetite was gone, drowned in wine and memories. "Thank you for dinner, Thomas. It was delicious, but I don't have much of an appetite."

"Jan," Susan called.

"Let her go," Thomas whispered as Janis left the room. "She needs a minute."

The last thing Janis heard as she headed down the hall was Susan sniffling. That pitiful sound—small, broken, too soft for someone who always seemed to steal everything—was like a needle in her skull. Closing the bedroom door, she banged her head against it—once, twice, and then a third time. The dull thud echoed in her head, grounding her in something physical, something real. She spun and stalked to the bathroom, slamming that door, too, not caring if they heard it. Let them. Let them sit there with their pity and their wine and their shocked little faces. The rage in her eyes was intense.

In the harsh overhead light, her reflection hit her like a punch. Her chest rose and fell in uneven bursts. Her pupils were wide, her cheeks flushed, her hair wild from the bun she'd hastily let down.

But it was the rage in her eyes that startled her most.

Unfiltered. Undeniable. Raw.

Susan was ruining everything. And Thomas? He'd laughed at her, too. Why would he do that? Why wouldn't he defend her? Wasn't he supposed to be on her side?

She hadn't asked for much. A sip of wine. A kind word. A moment of validation. Instead, they'd turned her into a joke. A scene. And all because she'd made a face when tasting something bitter.

Idiots. They could have left her alone, and she wouldn't have spilled her drink. She wouldn't have said something so stupid. That word clawed its way through her mind. *Stupid*. That's what they'd all think now. The poor unhinged twin. The one who couldn't handle a sip of Cabernet without reliving a murder.

Susan had already suggested therapy. Now, she'd handed them the proof they'd been waiting for. Talking about Eunie's blood like it was something fascinating.

The thought made something deep in Janis twist, tight and painful. Her lips peeled back in a silent snarl as she threaded her fingers into her hair and pulled—hard. The sting on her scalp grounded her, kept her from screaming. Kept her from losing it entirely. The pain was clean. Manageable. Unlike everything else.

Everything had been going so well. Thomas had been attentive. Protective. *Hers*.

And then everything had started to unravel. Not when she spilled the wine. Not when she said too much. It had started the moment her mother *survived*.

That single miscalculation threatened everything. She should have made certain. Should have watched the light leave her mother's eyes. But she hadn't. A wave of panic crested over her, cold and prickling against her skin, and for a moment she thought she might drown in it.

But then—oddly—it gave her clarity.

Of course she was panicking. That's all it was. Panic. A normal reaction to a temporary setback.

Janis gripped the edge of the sink until her knuckles turned white, then forced herself to inhale and exhale. Deep. Measured. She could hear the hum of the overhead light, the soft creak of pipes in the wall. She focused on those sounds until she calmed herself.

Soothing her hair down with trembling hands, she looked back into the mirror.

If she fell apart now, everything else would crumble with her. She wasn't about to let that happen. Not after how far she'd come. Not after what she'd done.

Eunie was dead.

Her mother—well, she wouldn't make the mistake of

leaving things to chance again.

And Susan . . . Susan had always played the innocent one. The kind one. The beloved one. But really, she was only another smiling face hiding a sharp edge. And now she was in Janis's way.

Not for long. She would find a way to make Thomas see Susan wasn't right for him. And once he did, there would be *nothing* standing between Janis and Thomas. He would see her. *Really* see her. He'd finally understand what they could be. What they *should* be.

She had to stay calm. Stay composed. Be smart.

No more mistakes.

With a final deep breath, she dabbed at her cheeks, patted her hair back into place, and blinked until her reflection softened.

Janis smiled. A smile that didn't quite reach her eyes.

"Everything's going to be okay," she whispered to her reflection. "One way or another."

Chapter Twelve

For what felt like the hundredth time, Janis tugged at the neckline of the black dress she'd borrowed from Susan. The material pinched at her ribs and clung across her chest. It wasn't uncomfortable in the traditional sense—it was suffocating in a way that made her feel exposed.

She had mentioned going home to find something that fit her, but Susan insisted Janis could borrow something. Always insisting. Always knowing best.

"We're the same size," Susan had said with a warm smile.

They weren't. Not in the ways that mattered.

Janis shifted again, the edge of her bra peeking out from the too-tight neckline.

"Perhaps a cardigan," Susan suggested when she noticed Janis shifting the material again.

"Yes," she stated flatly, "perhaps."

"I can get you—"

"I know where they are," Janis stated before pushing

herself up from the table.

The chair scraped loudly against the tile, jarring in the otherwise quiet room. Susan blinked, taken aback, but didn't say anything.

Janis didn't care. Her stomach was already a twisted mess of nerves. Not because of grief, not really. She was glad Eunice was being buried today. The world felt lighter with her six feet under. No, what had her unsettled was the way Thomas had doted on Susan all morning—preparing her toast the way she liked, brushing crumbs from her collarbone with tender fingers, pressing lingering kisses to her temple like she might shatter from the weight of the day.

Janis was burying her sister, too. But where was her tea? Where was her toast? Where were her kisses? Why wasn't anyone looking after her? Why wasn't *he*?

The unfairness of it all simmered like bile in the back of her throat. Every soft murmur and gentle gesture Thomas gave to Susan felt like a fresh cut. And Janis was bleeding, ignored in a dress that didn't fit.

Janis yanked Susan's closet open and shifted the hangers aside, as she'd done the night before. This time, her fingers settled on a black sweater with flat mother-of-pearl buttons. It was soft, understated—appropriate for a funeral, even if the woman wearing it wasn't truly mourning.

She slid the sweater on, buttoned it to her throat, and turned toward the vanity. It was such a delicate space—Susan's lotions, lip balms, neatly arranged brushes, and curated perfumes like something out of a magazine.

And then she looked into the mirror.

She didn't look tired. She didn't look grief-stricken. In fact, she didn't look like Janis at all.

Her skin, once pale and dull, now seemed luminous. Her lips were naturally flushed, her eyes clear. There was something alive in her gaze. Not joy. Not love. Power. It was power.

And while she didn't look beautiful like Susan, she looked *right*.

This wasn't the Janis who shrank in Eunice's shadow or stumbled over her words in front of Thomas. This Janis stood taller. She didn't beg for love—she expected it. She deserved it.

And if her sister had to be buried, her mother sedated, and Susan eventually nudged off the board?

So be it.

Janis tilted her head, admiring the sharpness of her cheekbones, the faint gleam in her eye. She didn't smile, not yet. But her reflection seemed to. As if the version of herself in the glass knew a secret the real Janis hadn't quite caught up to.

A heartbeat passed. Then another.

Confidence crept in like a spider—quiet and sure. A little bit unsettling.

She ran her fingers over a glass perfume bottle and lifted it to her nose. Not floral. Something warmer, muskier. She imagined Thomas burying his face in Susan's neck and inhaling this scent. The thought nearly made her throw the bottle across the room.

"Do you like that?" Thomas asked, startling Janis.

She felt the warmth of embarrassment heat her cheeks as she put the bottle down. "I do."

"I gave it to Susan the night before our wedding. She hasn't worn it yet. She said she's saving it for our first post-marital date."

His words stabbed at Janis.

She cleared her throat before saying, "I know you two weren't expecting to have company for so long. I really appreciate you letting me stay for a while."

The smile on his face fell as he put his hand on her upper arm. "We want you here. Honestly. It's best for everyone for us to be together right now."

His words brought the smile back to her face. *It's best for everyone for us to be together.*

"I think so, too," she whispered.

He slid his hand down her arm and gripped her hand. "There's something I've been meaning to speak to you about. I've been hesitant with everything that's going on. This is such a difficult time for you and Susan, but . . . I think there's something you should know."

Her heart nearly burst from her chest. "What is it?" she asked in the same hushed voice she'd used before. She couldn't find the strength to speak louder. The weight of her excitement was crushing down on her.

This was it. This was what she'd been waiting for. His confession. His admission that he felt the same for her as she'd felt for him from the moment they met.

Thomas lowered his face. Janis was searching for the words to tell him it was okay. She felt guilty, too, but she was certain that Susan would understand. She was certain they could make her understand they never meant to hurt her.

"You've been so brave through everything that has happened . . ."

"Well, you've done so much to help me. Asking the police to contact you and keeping Mom in line. I know that hasn't been easy."

"I want you to know, that even though you struggle to connect with people, I feel like—and please don't take this the wrong way—all of this has given us a chance to get to know each other better. I feel like we've overcome whatever awkwardness was between us."

Her heart faltered. A hollow ache settled deep in her chest. "There was never—"

This time his smile wasn't soft. It was patronizing. Warm, yet distant. Reassuring, but detached. Dear God, how she hated condescending smiles.

"There was," he insisted. "But I get it. I never took it personally. Susan explained how you've always been so quiet and shy. How hard it is for you to come out of your shell, but I've seen you starting to do better, despite the circumstances. I'm so glad you are finally feeling comfortable enough around me to relax and be yourself. I appreciate your trust, Jan. I really do. I wanted you to know that."

He squeezed her hand one last time, and the warmth of his touch might as well have been acid. She didn't say anything. Couldn't.

"Come on," he called from the hallway. "Let's finish breakfast. We're going to have a long day."

This time when his words rang through her ears, they didn't fill her heart with excitement. They filled her with resentment. She hid it behind a fake smile of her own. "Yes, unfortunately, it is going to be very long."

Janis swallowed, trying to fight the tears that were threatening to fill her eyes. She felt like a fool. Like an idiot. Like that stupid kid who had been so certain that her twin sister would be her best friend forever.

That nothing could come between them.

Until Eric Donner.

She'd had the biggest crush on him—since eighth grade. He was sweet, funny, always wore this beat-up jean jacket and smelled like cedarwood cologne. She'd saved a seat for him on the bus one morning in tenth grade, heart pounding in her chest, practicing what she'd say.

But he never showed up. Instead, at lunch, she'd seen him sitting beside Eunice—his arm already slung casually around her, his tray of fries between them. Eunice had laughed at something he whispered, then looked up and met Janis's gaze with a smirk that said *you never had a chance.*

Later that day, Janis had overheard Eunice bragging to her friends. "She actually thought he liked her. Poor Jan. So oblivious."

She hadn't cried that day. She'd gone numb. Stepped outside of herself. Like now.

Thomas had done the same thing, hadn't he? Led her to believe—no, *hope*—that she was special. That maybe, finally, someone saw her.

But he didn't. Not really. He never had.

Everyone betrayed her. Eventually.

And from now on, she'd remember that.

They entered the kitchen, and she sank down into her chair next to Susan.

"Jan," her sister said, "are you okay?"

"Yes, it's just . . ." She swallowed and sniffled as the tears she'd been fighting filled her eyes. "I'm sorry, Susan."

Susan gripped her hand, much like Thomas had done. "Don't apologize. Please. This has been such a hard time for all of us. We are all doing the best we can."

Janis nodded. "Thank you."

"Perhaps we could share our good news," Thomas

suggested.

Looking up, Janis questioned him with her eyes before looking at Susan.

Susan let out a childlike laugh. "Well, I suppose we could all use a little something to celebrate. I was going to wait until after the funeral, but I really need something for us all to look forward to."

Before the words were spoken, Janis realized what they were saying and a bit of her died. She felt Thomas slipping through her fingers. Or at least the illusion that she'd held that he could ever be hers. It was fading. Drifting away.

No. *Taken* away. Like everything she ever cared about.

"We're having a baby," Susan excitedly whispered. "We found out right before the wedding."

Janis's heart didn't quake. Didn't swell with happiness. It broke. The tears in her eyes dripped down her cheeks but she forced a smile. One of those fake smiles she'd always used to mask her misery. "Oh. How wonderful. How absolutely wonderful," she lied.

She'd lost him. There was no way he would choose Janis now. She'd lost him. She'd lost everything.

Chapter Thirteen

The funeral passed in a soft blur of organ music, white lilies, and hushed voices. People wept—some theatrically, some with genuine grief—and whispered about how young Eunice had been, how unfair, how sudden.

Janis stood next to Susan, who stood next to Thomas, who held her hand like they were the only two people in the world who'd lost someone. Whenever Susan's breath hitched, Thomas leaned down and murmured something into her ear. He rubbed her back. Brushed her hair off her shoulder. Kissed her temple.

Janis stood perfectly still, her hands clasped in front of her. No one whispered to her. No one kissed her temple.

After the graveside prayers and condolences, the mourners filtered toward the church hall next door for a small reception hosted by Eunice's congregation. Janis walked behind Thomas and Susan, far enough back that she didn't have to pretend she was part of them. She wasn't. Not really. Not anymore. Not ever.

Inside, folding chairs scraped against the floor and the smell of instant coffee and deli meat mingled with grief. Tables were covered in white plastic cloths. Desserts in Tupperware containers lined the wall.

Janis stood off to the side, near the coffee urn. Alone. Forgotten.

Susan and Thomas stood near the entrance, greeted like celebrities with smiles and hugs.

"You poor things," people said.

"Your honeymoon ruined."

"You two are so strong."

Janis could practically hear the capital letters in their voices. *You two.* Like they were one perfect unit. The grieving golden couple.

No one mentioned the woman who had shared a womb with the deceased. Who had watched her leave this Earth. No one asked how Janis was doing. A few people nodded politely as they passed, but no one stopped. No one lingered.

Her heart felt like it had been put in a blender. Not from grief over Eunice. No. Eunice could rot and Janis wouldn't shed a single tear.

But Thomas . . .

Thomas was holding Susan's hand as they accepted condolences. He was smiling—tiredly, humbly—like a hero. A good husband. A soon-to-be father.

And Janis? Janis was a footnote at her sister's funeral. The other twin. The one no one remembered. The one who had held Eunice's hand as she died. The one who had let her go.

She looked down at her black flats. Even her shoes felt

invisible.

Her sacrifice meant nothing. She'd let Eunice die. She hadn't called for help. She'd dragged her mother to bed and left her to suffer. All of it—for this. For Thomas. For a fantasy of belonging.

And they couldn't even be bothered to look at her.

She had given everything. And she was still alone.

Hours later, as mourners filtered out of the church fellowship hall and into the late afternoon sun, Janis found Susan and Thomas. "Would you mind taking me home for a bit? I want to check on the house. Make sure nothing's happened while we've been gone."

Susan looked concerned. "Do you want me to come with you?"

Janis forced a smile. "No, you should probably go home and rest, too. I'm sure you're tired . . . given your condition."

Susan glanced down at the black cotton hugging her still-flat belly. "I guess I am. Should we swing by and pick you up before we go to the hospital to see Mom?"

Janis froze. Her heartbeat thundered in her ears. She hadn't thought they'd go see Phylis today. She didn't want to go. Not now. Not after all this.

But she couldn't say no. Not without raising suspicion.

"Yes," she said, "that's fine."

Thomas gave her that familiar smile—gentle, polite, meaningless—and then turned his attention back to Susan. "Will you be okay if I leave you here for a bit while I run Jan home? I'll head right back."

"That's perfect," Susan said. She kissed her husband and returned to scanning the crowd as if Janis had already left.

Thomas led Janis to the car. Neither of them spoke as they got in. The car was too quiet, too sterile. The seats smelled like lemon cleaner and Susan's perfume.

Janis stared out the window. The city passed in blurs. People walking, talking, laughing. Living. The world had no idea what she'd sacrificed.

And for what?

"I'm sorry today was hard," Thomas said, eyes still on the road.

She almost laughed. *Sorry*. As if his pity made anything better. Something shifted in her as she stopped pretending. Stopped hoping. Stopped caring.

She looked at him—really looked—and every feeling she'd had for him curdled.

His kindness had been a lie. His sweetness a mask. His affection fake. He was exactly like the rest of them.

Eunice had taken her first breath before Janis ever got the chance to exist.

And from the moment she was born, Susan had taken what little attention had been given to Janis.

And Thomas? He'd taken what little Janis had left.

She gripped her purse tighter and pressed her nails into her palms. She didn't want him to touch her. Didn't want his words or his comfort. Didn't even want his attention anymore.

She hated him.

She hated them all.

A hate that burned so bright, it lit up the parts of herself she'd never dared to look at before. The parts that didn't need approval. That didn't need permission. The parts that didn't want love, only retribution.

By the time they pulled into her driveway, her smile was back—but it wasn't the mask she used to wear.

It was something new.

Sharper. Clearer.

"We'll see you soon," Thomas said as she opened the door.

She didn't answer as she closed the door. She walked up the sidewalk, listening to the engine hum behind her, waiting until it faded down the street.

She didn't wave.

She didn't look back.

The house loomed in front of her. Empty. Quiet. Hers.

And for the first time in her life, Janis welcomed the silence like an old friend.

The drive home was short, too short. She'd barely had time to imagine all the ways things could have been different. If Thomas had kissed her head. If someone—anyone—had reached for *her* hand. If Eunice hadn't sucked the air out of every room, and if their mother hadn't spoon-fed Eunice's ego from the day they'd been born.

The house was cold when she walked in. Not physically, but spiritually. The air was thick with silence. Stale. Her footsteps echoed too loud on the hardwood.

She dropped her purse by the door and stood there, the keys still in her hand, as if she'd forgotten what to do next.

This was her home. Her life. The place she'd kept in order, day after day, while everyone else got to go out and live theirs.

She walked through the house slowly. Past the living room where her mother's afghans were folded into a neat pile. Past the hallway where Eunice once told her she'd never find someone who could love her "with that face." Past the bathroom where she'd helped clean up her mother's messes after one too many bad days.

She ended in the kitchen. The heart of the home. A heart that had never beat for her.

Janis stood at the sink, staring at the spotless counter. The kettle was still sitting on the stove, its handle turned slightly to the right. That detail—so stupid and small—made her throat tighten. She hadn't even made tea the morning they'd left. She hadn't had time.

She didn't cry. That would have required more feeling than she had left.

Instead she laughed a bitter, strangled sound. Then she grabbed the empty fruit bowl and hurled it at the wall.

The crash was glorious. Final. Like a cymbal announcing the beginning of something.

She didn't stop there.

Picture frames, candles, vases, dishes. They all fell one by one like dominoes, casualties of the chaos that had been fermenting inside her for years. For *decades*.

She didn't scream. She didn't sob.

She simply destroyed. Silently. Meticulously.

And when the rage finally simmered into exhaustion, she sat on the kitchen floor, surrounded by broken glass and cracked ceramic, her hands bleeding from one of the picture frames she'd thrown.

The silence returned, but it was different now. Less suffocating. More like clarity.

Her mother. Eunice. Even Susan. They'd all lied to her. Used her. Mocked her. Betrayed her.

She sat in the wreckage of the kitchen, blood on her

palm, porcelain shards at her knees, and felt nothing.

No grief. No regret. No guilt.

Everyone who had ever mattered to her had betrayed her. She had given them her loyalty. Her care.

And they gave her silence in return.

Well, not anymore.

Slowly, she stood and walked to the sink, running her injured hand under cool water. The sting grounded her. Focused her.

She didn't need their love. Not Susan's fake smiles or Thomas's hollow kindness. And she certainly didn't a damn thing from her mother.

Janis dried her hands, wrapped her wound in a dish towel, and looked around at the wreckage. This was good. This was necessary.

Everything could be rebuilt.

But only once the rot had been cleared away.

Like a robot, Janis stepped around the shards of glass to the closet where she retrieved the broom and dustpan. As she swept up her mess, she imagined she was clearing away the past—the hurtful words, the dismissive attitudes. She was brushing it all away so she could start with a clean slate.

A stronger foundation.

And, more than anything, a clearer frame of mind.

Chapter Fourteen

The hospital smelled like antiseptic and grief.

Susan clutched Thomas's hand like a lifeline, walking so close to him they might as well have been sewn together. Janis trailed a few paces behind. As always. Out of step. Uninvited, but unavoidable.

Outside Phylis's room, a nurse stepped into their path.

"She's resting," the nurse said gently. "We've had to keep her sedated. Every time she wakes, she becomes agitated—screaming, crying. Her vitals spike. The doctor ordered continuous sedation to keep her stable."

Susan gasped, her free hand flying to her chest. "Oh no . . ."

"She's physically stable," the nurse assured her. "But emotionally, she's not there yet."

Susan nodded solemnly. "Can we sit with her?"

"Of course. Try to keep the noise down."

Inside, the room was dim and unnervingly still. Phylis lay slack and silent beneath a thin hospital blanket, her mouth slightly open, her face waxy and loose.

Susan went straight to the bed, took her mother's limp hand in both of hers, and began murmuring words of comfort—like the sedated woman could hear her.

Thomas hovered near the door, awkward and unsure. A fixture, not a participant. Now that she thought about it, she could recall many times when he'd stood back as if he didn't want to be there. She'd always put him on a pedestal, too high to even see for herself that he wasn't the slice of perfection she'd made him out to be. His wife was going through hell and he couldn't be bothered to comfort her. Definitely not the hero she'd seen even a week ago.

Janis didn't approach the bed. She drifted toward the window and stared out at the parking lot below. Rows of cars. People coming and going. Living.

"She doesn't look good," Susan said quietly.

Janis didn't turn. "She never did."

Susan frowned. "Jan . . ."

"I only meant she looks small. Frail." Janis finally turned, eyes wide with innocence. "It's strange, isn't it? Seeing someone who always seemed so powerful suddenly look so breakable."

Susan dropped her gaze to their mother. "She's been through a lot."

"We all have," Janis murmured. Then, a little louder—loud enough for Thomas to hear—"Some more than others."

He glanced at her but said nothing.

Janis moved across the room and gently rested a hand on Susan's back—mimicking the comforting gesture she'd seen Thomas perform a dozen times. "You're doing so well, Susan. Honestly. Better than I expected."

Susan turned, only enough to look at her older sister, eyes narrowed. "What do you mean?"

Janis smiled faintly. "I guess I'm worried. With the baby and everything. The stress. You know how fragile you used to be."

Susan's posture stiffened. "That was a long time ago."

"Of course," Janis said quickly, voice softening. "Still, I remember how hard it was for you. After Dad died. You could barely get out of bed. I made your toast the way you liked—crisp edges, soft center—but you would sit there and stare at it until I took it away."

Susan's mouth pressed into a tight line. "I was *eight*."

"Grief doesn't care about age," Janis murmured. "Some people simply feel things deeper. I've always admired that about you. How open you are with your feelings."

Susan looked unsure—about Janis, about herself.

Janis pressed on, her tone dipped in concerned affection. "With everything going on, I guess I'm a little worried history might repeat itself. There's so much pressure. A baby. Mom. Eunie . . ."

"I'm stronger now," Susan said, a little too fast.

"I know," Janis said, squeezing her sister's hand. "But even strong people have their limits."

Her gaze slid to Thomas, who stood a few feet away, scrolling through his phone.

Lowering her voice enough, she added, "That's why I'm so glad he's here. I really don't know what you'd do without him."

Susan didn't respond. She didn't have to.

Janis watched the flicker of doubt settle behind her sister's eyes and let the silence stretch. Planting seeds took patience. She turned back to the window, folding her arms. On the surface, she looked calm. Inside, her mind ticked like a clock wound too tight.

Eunice was gone—for good.

Phylis was sedated—for now.

And Susan? Susan would come apart. Janis would see to it. Thomas hadn't looked at her once since they'd arrived. That was fine. She didn't want his attention anymore.

She wanted *justice*.

After watching Susan and Thomas soak up sympathy like they were the only ones who'd lost something. Like Janis hadn't buried her twin. Like she hadn't sacrificed everything for nothing. She was done playing the quiet one.

"What happens if she doesn't get better?" Susan whispered.

Janis turned. "What do you mean?"

"I mean what if this is permanent? The sedatives. The confusion. What if she never really comes back?"

Janis tilted her head. In her mind, she was already planning. A pillow, maybe. Simple. Clean. Quiet. Or a bubble in the IV line—barely traceable. A little misstep in the tubing.

She could get her hands on a syringe. She could learn the nurse's rotation. She could time it. She could do it right.

Her mother wouldn't get the chance to turn on her again.

Janis brushed her finger lightly across Phylis's wrist.

Still warm. Still breathing. For now.

"She's going to be okay," she whispered. Loud enough for Susan to hear. "She's too stubborn not to be, right?"

Thomas smiled as he put his hands on Susan's shoulders, returning to the conversation. "Right."

Janis nodded. She would take care of everything. Every problem. Every loose end.

Starting here.

"Yes," she said, her tone mocking concern and sincerity. "Everything is going to be all right."

The drive back to Susan's condo was quiet. Not strained, not tense—just quiet in that brittle, overly polite way that meant everyone was thinking too much but saying nothing.

Janis sat in the back seat, her hands folded neatly in her lap like a well-behaved child. She didn't speak, but she didn't need to. Her silence had weight. Gravity. Every so often, she would glance at Susan in the rearview mirror and catch her sister's tired, distant expression. She was falling apart. Slowly. Carefully.

Exactly as Janis intended.

When they got back to the condo, Susan went straight to the bedroom to lie down. "I need a few minutes," she said with a wan smile.

Thomas kissed her forehead. "I'll make you some tea."

As soon as the bedroom door clicked shut, Janis moved to the kitchen counter and leaned casually against it. "She's really struggling."

Thomas turned from the kettle. "She's going to be okay, Jan."

Janis kept her voice level but laced it with the tiniest amount of tremble, enough to sound vulnerable. "I worry about her. And now with the baby . . . Stress can do awful things to pregnant women."

Thomas studied her, wary. "She's stronger than she looks."

"Maybe," Janis said with a small smile. "But she always did lean on other people when things got tough. You know, after Dad died, she didn't leave her bed for almost a month. Mom said I had to be the strong one."

Thomas frowned. "She was a kid."

"I was a kid, too," she said gently. "But I didn't get to break. I had to be the steady one. All I'm saying . . ." She trailed off and gave him a rueful look. "She needs you, Thomas. More than ever."

"I know that," he said. "That's why I'm here."

Janis lowered her gaze, tucking a strand of hair behind her ear. "Of course. You're good like that."

The tea kettle shrieked, sharp and sudden, and Thomas turned away. As he busied himself with mugs and honey, Janis moved to the fridge and took out a container of leftover soup she'd made earlier in the week. "I'll bring her some food."

"Thanks," Thomas said, distracted.

Janis glanced at him as he left the room. She focused on reheating the soup and picking the right bowl to serve it in. The right spoon for Susan to sip from. Then she carried the tray back to the bedroom, gave a gentle tap on the door, and stepped inside. Susan sat up, eyes puffy, cradling her stomach instinctively.

"I thought you might be hungry," Janis said, setting the tray down. "I reheated soup for you."

Susan blinked at the bowl. "Thanks."

Janis sat beside her on the edge of the bed, angled so she could watch her sister's expression. "I'm worried, that's all. You've been so pale lately. And tired."

Susan picked at the corner of the blanket. "It's a lot. Today was a bit too much."

"I know." Janis reached out and placed a hand over Susan's. "And Mom being sick isn't making it easier."

Susan sighed. "No. She never does."

"You don't have to take it all on," Janis whispered. "Not alone. You have Thomas, of course, but he's only one person. And he's already worried about you."

Susan looked over at her. "He said that?"

Janis gave her a sympathetic nod. "He didn't have to. I can tell. I think he feels like he has to carry both of us sometimes. But I don't want to be a burden."

"You're not a burden."

Janis smiled, touched her sister's hair. "You've always been the kind one, Susan. You see the best in everyone. But I'm not blind. I know when I've overstayed my welcome."

"No. You haven't."

"It's okay," she said quickly. "Really. You're the important one. You and the baby. That's what matters now."

Susan looked down, tears pooling in her eyes. "I don't know what I'd do without you."

Janis kissed her cheek. "You won't have to find out." She stayed with her sister a few minutes longer, brushing her hair back with gentle, practiced strokes.

And when she left the room, she found Thomas standing at the end of the hall. She met his eyes and gave him the sweetest smile she could conjure. "She needs rest. That's all."

He nodded slowly. "She's lucky to have you."

Janis's heart fluttered, but not with affection. With triumph.

He trusted her.

And trust, Janis was learning, was necessary to break someone.

Chapter Fifteen

The house had been silent for over an hour. A still, uneasy kind of silence. The kind that came after a storm. Janis moved through the hallway on quiet feet, carrying a folded blanket to the linen closet. Thomas's voice—low, deliberate—stopped her.

She didn't mean to eavesdrop, not really. But she paused outside his office door, holding her breath.

"I don't know," he said. "Some days, I feel like we're holding on by threads."

Silence. A pause. The faint sound of someone on the other end of the line. Then Thomas again. "No, I haven't told her that. I can't—not with everything that's going on."

Another pause.

"Of course I still love her. But there are things she didn't tell me. Things I deserved to know before committing to marriage."

Janis didn't hear the rest. The quiet gasp behind her pulled her attention away. Susan stood a few inches from her, frozen in place. She'd heard it, too.

For a moment, Janis thought Susan might say something. Scream. Storm into the office. But instead, her eyes filled with unshed tears as she lurched forward.

Straight into Janis's arms.

Caught off guard, Janis stumbled slightly but dropped the blanket and wrapped her arms around her sister with slow, steady purpose.

Susan trembled in her grasp. "He doesn't believe in us anymore," she whispered, voice cracking. "He thinks we're falling apart."

Janis stroked her hair, kept her voice low and warm. "You're going through so much. It's not your fault."

"I thought we'd be stronger than this," Susan said between gasping breaths. "I thought he'd fight harder."

Janis held her tighter. "Maybe he doesn't know how. Maybe he's tired, too."

Susan pulled back slightly, her face blotchy and red. "What am I going to do if he gives up?"

Janis brushed the hair from Susan's face and looked into her eyes.

"You don't have to do anything," she said. "You have me. And the baby."

Susan's breath hitched.

"I'll be here, no matter what Thomas decides. I'll help you through this. You're not alone."

Susan sagged into her again. Janis held her sister's weight with practiced ease, the way she used to hold her dolls as a child—gently, but with complete control. She guided Susan down the hall, away from the office door, away from Thomas's voice, away from the truth.

They sat together in the living room, Susan curled

up against her, still trembling. Janis let the silence stretch, carefully calculating the next thing to say. She didn't want to push too far. Not yet.

"I don't think Thomas meant to hurt you," Janis added gently. "He's probably overwhelmed. People say things when they're scared."

"But he didn't say it to me," Susan said. "He said it to someone else."

Janis said nothing for a moment. "Maybe that's because he didn't want to hurt you. Maybe it's easier to be honest with strangers than with the people you love."

Susan blinked, clearly unsure how to feel about that. Her fingers curled protectively around her stomach, a gesture Janis didn't miss.

"How far along are you?"

Susan hesitated. "Almost eight weeks."

She brushed her fingers against Susan's arm. "You're going to be an amazing mother."

"I don't feel amazing," Susan admitted. "I feel sick. I'm tired all the time. And I don't know if my husband even wants to stay married to me."

Janis took her hand. "You don't need him. You have me. No matter what."

Susan looked at her through bleary eyes. "Thank you for not being mad at me after my outburst."

"I can't be mad at you. You're my sister."

But the truth, the deeper truth, curled warm in her chest like a secret. She wasn't being kind. She was watching it all crumble. The marriage. The trust. The illusion of their happy little life.

All she had to do now was wait for the crack to widen.

That night, Janis lay in the guest bed, the covers pulled up to her chin, a gentle smile dancing across her lips. The room was dim, the soft glow of the nightlight casting faint shadows across the wall. Everything felt still, suspended—like the final inhale before something shatters.

From across the hall came muffled voices rose and fell only to rise again. The words were indiscernible, but the tone told her everything she needed to know. Sharp. Bitter. Panicked.

Susan and Thomas were fighting.

It was the kind of argument that didn't end in apologies and reassurances. It was the kind that left bruises, not on the skin but in the space between two people. It was the kind that changed things.

Janis closed her eyes and listened, her heartbeat slow and steady. The low hum of tension vibrated through the house.

A door slammed.

She tensed.

Footsteps. Quick. Heavy. Headed straight for her room.

Janis closed her eyes, softened her face, and slowed her breathing. She lay perfectly still, feigning the peace of sleep.

"Jan?" came her sister's emotion thickened voice. The mattress dipped as Susan crawled in beside her, curling against her back like a child seeking safety in the dark.

Janis didn't speak at first. Then Susan pressed her forehead into Janis's shoulder and let out a shuddering breath.

"What's wrong?" she asked with faux concern.

"Everything's terrible," Susan whispered. Her voice was raw, stripped of pretense.

Janis stayed still for a moment longer, then shifted enough to wrap her arm around her sister, pulling her in close. "Shh," she said, stroking Susan's hair. "It'll be okay. Everything will be fine."

Susan let out another tremble of breath and clung to her like a life raft.

Janis closed her eyes again—not to sleep, but to bask in the intimacy. The need. The quiet, desperate trust that only comes from someone whose foundation is beginning to crack.

She could feel it in Susan's touch. It wasn't a hug. It was a surrender.

The dependency was delicious.

The life Susan had built, the perfect one Janis had always been forced to admire from a distance, was crumbling faster than she could have imagined. Maybe it had never really been perfect at all. Maybe it had always been brittle underneath the gloss—like Thomas himself. Pretty on the outside, but hollow inside.

Maybe Janis hadn't broken anything.

Maybe she'd revealed the truth.

She hadn't destroyed Susan's life. She'd rescued her from it. From the pressure of perfection, from the silent disappointments and the surface-level smiles. From a marriage that had been rotting quietly beneath the surface before it had even begun.

She wasn't the villain here. She was the lifeboat. The one person who had shown up and stayed. The only one who truly understood.

Her lips curved.

She had always known how to love broken things.

The next morning, the kitchen was unusually quiet.

Janis sat at the table, her hands wrapped around a lukewarm mug of tea. The steam had long since stopped curling into the air. Outside, the early morning light was pushing through the blinds, casting faint lines across the floor.

Across the room, Thomas moved in clipped, mechanical motions—grabbing a travel mug, tucking his lunch into a neat canvas bag. His jaw was tight. His silence louder than any argument.

Susan busied herself slicing fruit. Her presence was as heavy as the unspoken tension between them.

Janis didn't speak. She didn't need to. The fracture was already there, stretching wide and silent.

Thomas turned and eyed Janis. "Do you want me to take you home on my way to work?" His voice was flat, but the question wasn't empty. It was laced with something unspoken.

Janis lifted her brows slightly. "I can call a car. It's no trouble."

Susan turned from the sink. "I can take care of my sister," she said, her voice quiet but sharp.

Thomas's mouth twitched, but he didn't look at her. "I'm not so sure anymore."

The words dropped like a stone into the room. No one moved.

Janis looked at Susan, who suddenly seemed impossibly small in the morning light. Her shoulders slumped. Her eyes glossy with unshed tears. The steel from earlier had drained out of her. What was left looked tired. Lost.

Thomas slung his bag over his shoulder and headed for the door without another word.

The door clicked shut behind him.

Susan didn't speak. She stood there, her arms still crossed, as if trying to hold herself together.

Janis took a sip of her tea. It was bitter. But the moment was sweet. Yes, it was time to go home. Her work here was done.

Chapter Sixteen

The hospital elevator dinged, and the doors slid open. Susan had insisted they stop at the hospital before taking Janis home.

Janis's heart dropped to her feet when she spotted their mother's doctor talking with two police officers and a casually dressed man in khakis and a red plaid shirt. The doctor noticed them and said something. The police turned toward the elevator and Janis's stomach filled with a million marching ants.

"Oh no," Susan gasped. She gripped Janis's hand and took a step, but Janis was rooted in place. She couldn't move. Panic engulfed her, much like she'd felt when the thug in Mexico pulled a knife on her and Eunice.

With a tug, Susan pulled Janis from where she stood and out of the elevator car. Her mind was racing nearly as fast as her heart.

"What's going on?" Susan demanded.

"Which one of you is Janis Duke?" one of the officers asked.

Susan turned to Janis who simply stared in response to the question.

"She is," Susan answered. "I'm her sister."

"Susan Hayward," the same officer clarified.

"Yes."

The strange man in plaid gestured toward the hallway to the left. "There's a room where we can sit and have some privacy. Right this way."

Janis could barely hear Susan questioning the doctor. Her heart was thumping so hard she could barely hear anything at all. The walls were closing in on her. She'd done a bad thing and now she was in trouble.

They walked into a neutral-colored room with a long table in the middle. The stranger had suggested they all sit. Everyone did except for the police officers who stood at the front of the table, clearly trying to command dominance of the group.

"Ms. Duke," the plaid man said, "my name is Aaron Martinez. I'm a grief counselor here at the hospital."

Susan gasped but the man shook his head slightly.

"Your mom is fine," he said reassuringly.

"Your mother is awake," the same police officer who had done all the talking so far said. "She's made some pretty serious accusations against you, Ms. Duke."

"Against Janis?" Susan asked, shocked.

"Can you tell us what happened the night she had her heart attack, specifically around the time you and your mother went to bed?" the officer asked.

Janis shifted. "Um. Nothing out of the ordinary, really. I didn't have anything suitable for the funeral, so Susan let me try on a few dresses from her closet. I chose one and then we sat down for dinner. It was later than usual because we'd been so busy finalizing the funeral plans. We had to bring Eunie home from Mexico which took a few days, so her husband had done everything but choose the casket. He asked us to help with that. It had been a long day. Mom and I went to bed early."

"Did you argue?" the officer asked.

Janis let her shoulders sag. "Not exactly argue, but we did exchange a few words."

"Were you aware your mother was having a cardiac episode?" the officer asked.

Susan spoke up. "Our mother has a tendency to exaggerate her symptoms. We've all become a little numb to her insistence that she isn't feeling well."

"Ms. Duke, were you aware that your mother wasn't feeling well?"

"She did say something, but like my sister said, she's been playing up her symptoms for sympathy lately. I didn't give her much attention."

"Did you tell her that you murdered your sister?"

Susan gasped and sat forward. "Our sister was stabbed during a mugging. The incident was caught by a surveillance camera."

"Did you tell your mother you refused her cries for help?"

"I-I didn't," Janis stammered out. "She was bleeding everywhere, there was no one around. I couldn't leave her there bleeding. What was I supposed to do?"

"Get help," the officer suggested.

"And leave my injured sister alone?" Janis looked at Susan. "I couldn't leave her like that."

"I know," Susan reassured her. Looking at the officer, she set her jaw. "If she'd tried to find help, our sister would have died alone on a dirty sidewalk. The medical examiner told the police there was nothing she could have done."

"Eunice was your twin, is that correct?" Aaron asked.

Janice looked across the table at him. "Yes."

"It had to have been horrible to see her go through that."

The sympathy in his eyes caused her to nod.

"It was," she agreed.

"I know it's only been a few days, Janis, but have you talked to anyone about what you went through?"

"The police in Mexico. My sister," she said gesturing toward Susan.

The officer who had been silent finally spoke. "Your mother says she told you she was having an episode, and you ignored her. She says you dragged her to bed and told her to go to sleep."

"Oh my God," Susan muttered. Her voice cracked as if she couldn't take much more.

Janis blinked. "We had a few words and I . . . I put her to bed and told her to get some sleep. I didn't drag her. I mean . . . Why would I drag her?"

"When you say you put her to bed, what does that mean?"

Susan started sobbing. That far too familiar sense of being alone and abandoned settled over Janis. Susan was proving to be as worthless as Thomas had been. Strong in appearance, but weak when it mattered.

Janis swallowed as she looked across the table at Aaron. He offered her the sweetest, most supportive smile she'd ever seen. A sense of peace calmed some of the panic rising in her chest.

Taking a slow breath, Janis found the strength to answer. "Well, every night I have to help my mother get ready for bed and tuck her in. A bit like a child," she said, hoping her resentment didn't show. "She likes to be cared for even when she doesn't need it and . . . well, I still live with her because she insists on it. Our father passed away decades ago, and Mom says she'll be too lonely living alone," she said glancing at Susan. Frowning, she returned her attention to Aaron. "She expects me to put her to bed. And I did so that night like every night."

The police didn't seem moved by her answer. She might not have had a lifetime of interacting with law enforcement, but the little she'd gained in the last week and a half had convinced her that even if they were sympathetic to her plight, they wouldn't have let on. They tended to remain flat and unreadable.

The talkative officer narrowed his eyes a bit. "But you weren't concerned that she was having a medical crisis?"

"No," Janis stated. "I was irritated with her because I'm grieving, too, but she's only concerned about herself, and I wanted her to go to bed so I could have some quiet time." She was surprised at the tears that filled her eyes. She hadn't expected that, but she was glad they had appeared. She felt it made her statement seem genuine. "We didn't fight, per se, but I did tell her that I was tired, and we both needed to get some rest."

"Mrs. Hayward," the first officer said, "have you seen anything that would cause concern regarding the way your sister treats your mother?"

Susan wiped her eyes and then shook her head. "Janis is a saint for all she has to put up with. I've been very caught up in my own life and Eunice was as well. Caring for Mom has been Janis's responsibility and she's done it without complaining once. I can't believe that woman has done this."

"Do you think she's lying?" the second officer asked.

"Yes, I do. I think she's desperate to get attention," Susan said. "Just the other night, Janis told her to get her own glass of water but the way our mother acted, you'd think Janis had shoved her out of a moving vehicle. To say our mother is dramatic would be a vast understatement."

"Have you ever lost your temper with your mother?" Aaron asked.

"Janis doesn't have a temper," Susan stated flatly. "Look, we've had a long week. We buried our sister and our mother was hospitalized. Is this really necessary?"

"Your mother accused your sister of elder abuse," Aaron said. "The medical staff is legally required to report such claims, and the police are obligated to check them out."

The second police officer said, "I think we've heard all we need to."

"We'll follow up if we have any further questions," the first officer said.

Once they left, Susan sat back and shook her head. She snatched a tissue from the box on the table and dabbed at her eyes. "Of all the ungrateful things our mother has done." She frowned as she looked at Janis. "Honey, I am so sorry she did this to you."

"She's grieving, too," Janis said lowering her gaze and her voice for effect. "I'm sure she's confused about what happened."

"Don't make excuses for her," Susan said. "This is outrageous. Even for her."

"Janis," Aaron said with a warm tone that drew her

attention to him. The sympathy in his eyes turned into concern. "I'd like to ask you a few questions about your relationship with your mother if that's okay."

She simply nodded.

He shifted for a moment before meeting her gaze again. "Has your mother ever physically hurt you? When you aren't doing what she wants? Or playing into her need for attention?"

She hadn't. Her mother was manipulative and bullying. The kind who would make a child feel terrified but would never raise her hand to one. But Janis saw an opportunity and she wasn't going to miss it. She lowered her gaze to where her hands were clutched in her lap. "She's never been kind. I think Susan can attest to that. I remember once she locked me in the closet because . . . Well, I don't really remember why. Do you?"

Susan sniffled again before shaking her head. After a few moment, she asked with a quivering voice, "Has she hurt you, Jan?"

"She can be . . . harsh sometimes."

"But has she ever hit you or anything like that?" Aaron asked.

Fearing her lie would be exposed if she spoke, Janis simply twisted her lips, forced a look of embarrassment to her face, and then looked down.

"Oh no." Susan started sobbing again as she hugged her sister. "I'm so sorry. I didn't know."

"Grief can make people act in unexpected ways," Aaron offered.

Susan scoffed. "Yes, except our mother has always been this way. Always. Janis shielded me from her when we were younger. I suppose I . . . I didn't know how bad things were."

Janis heard Susan's declaration, but she was hanging on Aaron's words. Grief made people act in unexpected ways. Like . . . overly obsessing about her brother-in-law or allowing her mother to suffer a heart attack. It wasn't Janis who had done those things. It was her grief.

Her grief had made her do those things.

She was glad that Aaron saw that. That he understood.

Aaron jotted some notes in the folder that had been on the table in front of him. "I'm going to notify your mother's medical team that I don't believe the accusations she's made. Janis, I know you've been through a lot, but I'd like you to consider finding another place to live. Your mother is expected to make a full recovery. She won't need round-the-clock care. If you are able, I believe it would be in your best interest to relocate and put some distance between the two of you. If your mother does need more intensive care, we can find someone who your mother won't be able to abuse."

Abuse.

For the first time in her life, in all her years, someone finally said what Janis had known all along. She'd been abused. Her mother had abused her. Aaron had not only recognized it, but he'd said it out loud. He'd said in front of Janis and Susan that Phylis Duke was an abuser.

Something shifted in Janis. Something she'd never felt before. Aaron had seen her. He'd seen the pain she'd endured. He'd seen through her calm exterior to the hurt inside.

And he'd acknowledged it.

"You can stay with us. Whatever happens," Susan offered. "For as long as needed."

"Janis," Aaron continued, "how do you feel about that?"

She looked at him and blinked.

"About leaving your mother to live on her own," Aaron clarified.

"Oh." She looked at Susan. "I suppose it's time, isn't it? I've looked at apartments several times over the years, but I never got much further than that. It would be nice to have a quiet home to go to after work."

"I don't want you to worry about Mom at all," Susan said firmly. "I'm going to step in. I'll hire someone if needed. I want you to focus on healing and starting your own life. You deserve that after all these years."

"You can't, Susan. Not in your condition."

Susan glanced at Aaron. "I'm pregnant."

"Congratulations."

"Thank you," she said. Then her eyes filled with tears again. "I'm so sorry. I had no idea she was treating you so badly."

Aaron stood. "Susan, you'll help Janis find her footing?"

"Absolutely. I'm going to take care of her for a change." She hugged Janis. "It's going to be okay. I promise."

Aaron rounded the table and put his hand on Janis's shoulder as he looked into her eyes. The tenderness there stole her breath away. He dipped his head, making sure to meet her gaze, and smiled at her. "You've been through a lot. I would really like to help you through this, Janis. I'd like to help you process everything so you can move forward."

A smile curved her lips. "That would be nice."

"Here's my card." He held out a small rectangle with his name and number printed on it. "Please call me."

As she took the card, her fingers brushed against his and she felt a jolt all the way to her heart. "I will."

His smile grew. "Good. I'm looking forward to visiting with you again."

Janis looked at the card, read Aaron's name, traced the raised lettering.

"Try to get some rest. You've had such a long day," he said with a soft tone that rippled through her. Not only did his sweet words mend her heart, but they made it quake.

A gentle rumble that put all the pieces back into place.

A *heartquake*.

Acknowledgments

When I wrote this book, it was a short story, barely scratching the depth of Janis' spiral into obsession. I knew there was more to this story, but I wasn't in the right place to dig deep into those emotions. I put this book on a shelf, occasionally pulling it out and adding bits here and there or tossing it at various beta readers to get validation that it was worth writing.

Over the last few years, this developed from a little nugget of a "what if" story to what it is now and that is because of a long list of people.

Terry Boudreaux, Joey and Mark Jones, and Elaine Sapp—thank for you reading this, loving this, and pushing me to keep going.

Jaelan McCloud—you are just getting started as an editor, but the depth you bring to help authors enrich their characters is amazing. You will go far, and any author on the receiving end of your insights will be damn lucky.

Linda Robinson—you are and always will be a cherished friend, and your copyediting ~~ain't~~ *isn't* bad either. Thank you for always making time for me, my characters, and dishing out words of encouragement.

Shelly Lea—you have been with me through so many ups, and far too many downs. You've listened to me scream, cry, and helped me find light in the darkest of moments. You are more than an editor. You are a friend and a sister. I love you, not only for seeing me but for helping me take Janis, and all my other characters, to the next level.

About the author

Nestled in the enchanting expanse of the Midwest, Marci Wilson shares her humble abode with her seriously lucky husband and their menagerie of rescue pets.

Armed with a laptop in one hand and a margarita in the other, Marci spins tales that capture the imagination of her readers.

She is a multi-published author, a professional book editor and author coach, and co-owner of MaHanna Press.

When she isn't writing or traveling, she can usually be found rescuing animals or trying to convince her husband to try new culinary delights.

Visit her at https://marciwilson.com/

Also by Marci Wilson

Cloverton Romance Series

Going Home: Series Starter
Turn the Page: Book One
Faked With Love: Book Two
Music of the Heart: Book Three
In Full Bloom: Book Four
Tattered Dreams: Book Five
By Design: Book Six
A Cloverton Christmas (short story)
The Perfect Blend: Book Seven
A Healing Touch: Book Eight
Against the Grain: Book Nine

Coming Soon

Saving Grace

After a scandal destroyed her reputation, art professor Erin Hoffman is desperate for a second chance. A new job at Kenton College promises a quiet life far from the whispers and wreckage she left behind.

However, Conner Chapman, head of Kenton's art department, has other plans. With his easy charm—and the help of his poised, magnetic wife, Grace—he draws Erin into his social circle before she can stop him.

For the first time in years, Erin feels safe. Comfortable. Like she belongs.

Still, she's learned not to trust too easily. And the Chapmans' life? It feels *almost* too perfect.

She tells herself she's only being careful. But soon, she's watching. Noticing. Slipping into old habits she promised never to repeat.

She's been wrong before.

But what if this time... she's not the only one with something to hide?